G

The Hate Fighters

by Kathryn Dahlstrom

Good News Clubs®,
weekday Bible clubs for boys and girls,
are sponsored by
Child Evangelism Fellowship® Inc.

Published by

CEF PRESS®
P. O. Box 348
Warrenton, MO 63383-0348

2 3 4 5 6—01 00 99 98 97

ISBN 1-55976-832-0

To my brothers, who trained our family dogs into becoming animals we all loved.

Many thanks to:
The American Kennel Club
Coral Allenby, Dog Trainer
Dee Carfagna, the Dog Lady

Mrs. Peterson pushed her clear-rimmed glasses back up on her nose, gave her curly blond hair a shake and said, "All right, team one. You'll break the tie if you can all stand up and recite the verse."

Carlos Hernandez thrust up his hand, then spoke before he was called on. "Can we practice first?"

"You've got two minutes."

The kids on team one looked at each other with sharp gasps. "All right, you guys!" Carlos whispered, frantically beckoning his team closer. The other nine on his team shot out of their folding chairs and the battered metal gave its usual squeaks and scrapes. The teammates clustered around him. He started, and they all joined in with sharp whispers. "John fifteen, seventeen. 'This is my commandment—' "

His friend, Felipe (pronounced Fay-LEEP), cut them off. "No, man! *Command,* not commandment!"

"Oh, yeah. John fifteen, seventeen. 'This is my command: love each other.' John fifteen, seventeen."

The last three words of the verse were garbled. Some were saying "each other" and others were saying something else that Carlos couldn't make out.

"Ain't it 'love *one another'?"* put in Nathaniel Bronson. His nickname was Bronce and he was in sixth grade.

They looked at each other in desperation. They'd just started learning the verse this week and no one could remember which version was right, until a girl spoke up. She looked about Carlos' age—eleven—and she had straight black hair pulled back in a pony tail. She'd never been to a Good News Club meeting before, and she wasn't in his class. Maybe she didn't go to his school. He would have noticed because she was Japanese or Chinese or something like that, and there weren't that many of them at Fern Street Elementary.

"I've heard it as 'love one another,' " she said.

Team one turned to Carlos, who gave a frustrated shrug. "*I* can't remember, and we're out of time! Let's go with what she said. *Love one another*."

They stood. Team two, headed by Mashell (pronounced Muh-SHELL) Robertson and Carlos' thirteen-year-old sister Anna (AH-nuh), sat waiting with their arms crossed, daring them to get it right. "John fifteen, seventeen," team one recited. "'This is my command. Love one another.' John fifteen, seventeen."

Mrs. Peterson raised one eyebrow and glanced at her co-teacher, Mrs. Joyce, who gave a slight shake of her head. "That was *close.* There are other versions of the Bible that have the verse end that way. But I taught you the way it's written in the New International Version. And I said you had to get it exactly right, didn't I, Mrs. Joyce?"

The dark-skinned lady nodded.

"Sorry about that."

Team one groaned.

"Team two, your turn. If you get it *exactly* right, you win."

Team two gave each other exultant grins as they scrambled together to practice. Their whispers were easily loud enough for Carlos to know they had it perfect. He rolled his eyes and gave the new girl a sharp glance. She was staring straight ahead, sober faced. *If only I hadn't listened to her!* he scolded himself silently. *I knew the right way all along!*

Team two got the verse *exactly* right, of course. They whooped and clapped hands. Big deal! Winning just meant they got to draw something out of the "prize bag" first. Then the third teacher, Miss Lindstrom, called them one at a time to collect their snacks and drinks and leave. Which was even less of a deal because those with brothers or sisters on team two had to wait for them anyway.

It was just the losing part. Carlos *hated* losing. When Mrs. Peterson finally called on him, he passed the girl's chair without saying anything to her. No one spoke to her but the teachers. "We're glad you came today, Judy," Mrs. Peterson was saying. "Come back next week, okay?"

"Okay," she answered in a voice that didn't sound like she wanted to.

Carlos only had ten seconds to decide between a yo-yo and a paddle-and-ball. He snatched up the second of his two options and grabbed a bag of peanuts. But which juice box was he in the mood for? Grape or fruit punch? Grape . . . .

The new girl was outside already. She must have taken

a set of stickers. Miss Lindstrom kept those in her totally stuffed backpack. He followed her out and watched her pass Anna and Mashell, standing together on one of the many sidewalks that interlaced Gordon Brown housing community. They were busy talking and didn't notice her.

He wondered if maybe someone shouldn't say hi at least (after all, it wasn't completely her fault team one lost), when he was distracted by a royal blue pickup truck pulling up to the littered street curb. *Hey! Miss Lindstrom's boyfriend, Stan! He must be here to pick her up.*

The truck had a matching topper on the back. Carlos strained to see through its gray-tinted windows, hoping he'd catch sight of—

Yes! Movement! And a big, square, muzzled head and a broad chest and a long, upswept tail. Even if he hadn't started thundering out barks so deep and loud that the topper vibrated, there was no question who was back there.

Charlie, Stan's Great Dane!

Carlos grinned with delight. He loved his own golden retriever, Peppy, the best, of course. But he hadn't seen Charlie for months, and this Great Dane was one *cool dog*. Strong and big and fun. He ran to the rear window and put his hand on it so Charlie wouldn't feel alone.

Ka-*thunk!* The dog hit the back gate with his front paws so hard it rattled. Carlos took two steps back, out of sheer instinct. But Charlie was being purely friendly. He pawed the tiny gap between the topper window and the gate and whined with squeaky, high pitches completely different from the bass voice he barked with.

He wanted *out.* A crowd of kids had clustered around the truck by this time—Anna and Mashell; Bronce; another sixth-grader named Juan (pronounced Hwahn); an eight year old named Tony; Carlos' younger sisters Maria and Victoria; and Loeesha (pronounced Loe-EE-shuh), Mashell's five-year-old sister. "Nice doggy!" she said with a squeal.

Slam! Charlie hit the back gate again. Mashell gave an awed laugh. "That's one way to put it, girl!"

Stan climbed out of the cab and greeted the kids, who did the same to him. "I'm glad you brought Charlie. He's great!" said Carlos.

Stan grinned and gave his head a self-conscious toss. He had light brown, baby-fine hair, and his bangs kept wanting to drape down on his forehead instead of staying combed to the side. Anna leaned toward Mashell and whispered, "Doesn't he have the *bluest* eyes? And I like how he wears his hair . . . ."

She didn't think anybody else heard her. But Carlos rolled his eyes at Felipe and the two boys started snickering. So did Mashell. "Back off, girlfriend!" she teased. "He already claimed by Miss Lindstrom!" Her voice went loud and she directed her next words to Stan. "She gatherin' up her stuff."

"Oh. Thank you," said the young man, closing the truck door and heading toward the building.

Meanwhile, Anna's mouth had popped open and her face had turned as red as the blouse she was wearing. "*Mashell!* I—now *wait* a minute! I just think he's good looking! I didn't mean—I'd *never—*"

The more she tried to explain herself, the more flustered she grew. And the harder Carlos, Felipe and Mashell laughed. At that moment, Miss Lindstrom struggled out the meeting room door with her backpack slung across her shoulders, her arms laden with leftover snacks and her guitar, and her long auburn hair looking as unraveled as usual. She nearly ran into Stan, who tried to take a few things from her arms. Juice boxes and peanut bags hit the ground. Several kids rushed to help.

"Before we leave I have to let Charlie out for a little walk," Stan explained as he took the guitar from Miss Lindstrom's hand. Loeesha, who always listened to conversations nobody expected her to, blurted out, "Your doggy wants out? *I* can do it!"

"No, girl!" her big sister yelled. But Mashell was too late. Loeesha's hand shot up, caught hold of the gate handle and twisted it. It dropped with a metallic *bam* and the enormous dog surged out the opening. The little girl was too shocked at his size to pet him (the top of her head reached only to his chest!), and he was moving too fast for her to touch him anyway.

The kids screamed and yelled. Stan let out a bellow, thrust the guitar at Miss Lindstrom, then pelted after his dog, shouting at him to "Sit, come, stay, *heel!"* Charlie, ignoring everyone in his mad joy to be *free,* galloped down the sidewalk, nearly knocking over the new girl, Judy, who had paused for a look before continuing on by herself.

Oh, man! thought Carlos. It was bad enough that

Charlie was running loose. But he was loose here in Watts, Los Angeles, with its gangs and drug pushers and drive-by shootings. One of the most dangerous urban areas in the United States.

No telling what would happen if they didn't catch the dog right away.

Thank goodness there wasn't much traffic. Charlie scampered past row after row of Gordon Brown's blue and gray, two-story apartments. A crowd of big and little people pounded after him. Everybody was yelling, but Stan's stern, desperate commands carried over all. Curious people stuck their heads out doors and peered through windows to see what the racket was about. Had somebody started a riot?

All this only made the dog, already in a good mood, more excited. He bounded along, covering amazing chunks of ground with each leap, delighted with this game of tag.

He noticed a lady standing on her porch and made for her, assuming she wanted to play, too.

She didn't, and let the world know with a shriek as she scuttled for her front door. A man setting his trash cans on the curb picked up one of the metal lids and held it as though he was wielding a shield against this golden-brown monster. Charlie sailed past him with a happy snort.

He stopped for a quick second, long enough to sniff a bush but not long enough for his chasers to catch him. Carlos was getting worried. It was *fine* to watch him race around the quiet streets of Gordon Brown housing community. But what if Charlie decided to branch out into the rest of Watts? He'd cause a car accident. He'd get hit by a truck or something. He'd get killed.

The boy was getting an idea. They'd never catch him running like this. He was way too fast. What if they *lured* him to stop? With what, though? Food? He was probably too excited to be hungry. He wanted to *play.*

The answer hit him. Okay, get him a playmate. The boy turned and tore away in the other direction. "Where are you *going?"* Anna called after him.

"Home. I know a way to stop Charlie!"

Stan stopped running and doubled over, gasping smoggy air. *"How,* Carlos?"

"You'll see!" He didn't have the breath or the time to explain. Good thing his house was only two blocks away. The reason for his rushed trip home saw him coming from the backyard and greeted him with high-pitched yips and barks.

"Hey, Peppy!" he panted, jumping to the top of the back porch without touching the steps. His golden retriever's leash was kept on a nail beside the door. He reached in and got it without going inside, snapped it on Peppy's collar and was out of the yard again before Mama had even reached the porch.

"Where are you off to? And where are your sisters?" she demanded in Spanish.

"Chasing Charlie!" He didn't have time to explain more. She'd have to find out later who in the world Charlie was. He pelted back to Gordon Brown, hoping the dog hadn't traded its trash-lined alleys and patchy yards for more of Watts.

He and his chasers weren't anywhere in sight at the moment. The boy paused and heard distant squeals and shouts and once in awhile a deep-voiced *"Hrrooff!"*

Peppy perked up his ears. "Who's *that?* What do you *say,* dog?" Carlos asked him, hoping he'd get the message and answer back. It worked. These two dogs were friends, after all.

Peppy gave an excited squirm, huffed, and barked out

his "hi" greeting. Surely he recognized Charlie's voice, but more important, would Charlie recognize *his?* Carlos had his answer in a minute as he saw a mouse-sized (from this distance) brown dog rollicking toward him. People no bigger than grasshoppers ran after him.

But the "mouse" grew larger at an alarming rate. Soon Carlos wondered if this was such a good idea. Peppy was yipping and bobbing and begging his master to let him loose so he could join the romp, which made him hard to hold onto. Charlie barreled closer, grown now to roughly the size of a pony.

"*Whoa,* Charlie! Slow down, boy! *Stop!"* squeaked Carlos, backing up. Oh, *no!* Tackle time! The boy turned his back to this living freight train and covered his head with his free arm. But the Great Dane swept past him, then circled around. *Yank!* Carlos found himself spinning as Peppy bolted after his friend. The boy had two choices—run or lose his arm.

He ran. Then just like that, the chase was over. Charlie and Peppy stopped to sniff noses; and Stan, with sweat all over his flaming red face and his hair all messed up, staggered to Charlie and hooked his leash on his collar. "No, *no, NO! Bad*—dog! You *come* when—I tell—you to!"

Charlie didn't pay much attention to his bawling out. The young man soon ran out of air to yell with and doubled over again, panting between words. "Thanks—Carlos, for getting him to—stop. Good—thinking."

All the kids gathered around, petting the two dogs and pouring compliments on Carlos.

"You're a *brain,* man!" said Bronce.

"There's no way we were gonna catch him!" added Tony.

Mashell laughed. "Did you see the way Charlie made that lady *hightail* it?"

Miss Lindstrom had stayed with the chase, and she looked as exhausted as her boyfriend. "I'm just relieved he didn't get run over."

Stan moaned. "He could have been—shot, or he could have wrecked—something, or hurt somebody . . . ." He straightened up. "Saturday's obedience training class isn't coming any too soon."

"Class?" asked Carlos, perking up *his* ears this time. "For dogs?" He looked at his retriever and blurted out, "I always wanted to train Peppy. He'd be good at it, you know?" He gave the two young adults a hopeful glance.

"Do you think there'd be any way I could—" The boy cut himself off as reality set in. "Nah. I bet it costs money."

"Fifty dollars," said Stan.

The other kids groaned in sympathy. Miss Lindstrom scurried close to Stan and whispered something in his ear. He nodded and looked thoughtful. Then he grinned. "Yeah. Great idea, Becky! Carlos, it was your good thinking that let me catch Charlie, or there's no telling what he might have done. I think that's worth fifty dollars."

Carlos' mouth fell open. The other kids cheered. "I would have paid twice that as a reward if he'd gotten lost," the man continued, embarrassed.

Miss Lindstrom gave Charlie's broad neck a pat. "What if you hadn't gotten him back?"

"For *real?*" Carlos finally managed to blurt out. "I can bring Peppy to the class?"

"We'll pick you up at—" the two adults conferred back and forth, deciding a time—"ten o'clock in the morning."

"That'll be *great!*" The boy's voice was going higher, and he was speaking faster with each word. He felt giddy, like he could burst into laughter over anything.

"Let me buy a training collar for him," said Miss

Lindstrom.

Carlos would have hugged them both if his friends hadn't been watching. He said thank you at least a dozen times. Charlie and Peppy had calmed down enough for a fast walk back to Stan's truck. But Charlie did *not* want to go back inside, no matter how sharply his master commanded him to "Kennel!"

This was a problem. Stan couldn't just lift him. He was a cheerfully stubborn animal who happened to weigh one hundred fifty pounds! Stan tried luring him into the truck box with food. But the Great Dane wasn't a bit hungry. The young man resorted to lifting Charlie's front paws onto the back gate (which was lying flat), then tried to hoist up the dog's rear legs while Becky held his collar.

But Charlie mistook the whole thing for a wrestling game. He flopped his forepaws onto Miss Lindstrom's shoulders and licked her face. She gave a tight-lipped scream and turned away, which allowed the dog to wrench free from her grasp. He wriggled one leg loose and spun around, planting his paws on Stan's chest. But his master wasn't ready for it, and he toppled backwards. He wound up on his back, sprawled across the sidewalk, getting the same face wash his girlfriend got.

"*Kennel,* confound it!" the young man yelled in frustration, pushing Charlie away and sitting up to flick the dog saliva out of his hair.

Once again it was Carlos to the rescue. He got Peppy to kennel into the truck box, then when Charlie followed his friend in, the boy called his own dog back out, and Miss Lindstrom *quickly* slammed the gate shut while Stan held the new prisoner's collar. He closed the back window with a groan of relief. "I can't wait for that class," he muttered.

Neither could Carlos.

* * * * * * * *

Mashell walked Loeesha safely home, then told Grandma she was going to the store with Anna.

"You two ain't just gonna buy junk are you?" demanded the white-haired lady.

"Anna's mama wants her to get some milk an' some

chicken."

Grandma went to the closet and pulled out a tattered, vinyl purse. "They got ground beef on sale for ninety-nine cents. 'Bout time they give us a break on somethin'. Get us pound of it an' a dozen buns while you at it. An' some lettuce an' a tomato, too."

"We havin' burgers?"

"Mm-hmm."

"Got any chips to go with 'em?"

"Just bought a big bag at the dollar store."

Mashell made a face. "I hope they ain't stale like the last ones you got there."

She took the five-dollar bill from Grandma's knobby brown fingers.

"Instead of complainin', be glad we got money enough to buy food with."

"Can I get cookies or somethin' for dessert?"

"If you got enough. *After* you buy the meat an' vegetables."

Mashell hurried out before Loeesha could catch where she was going and beg to tag along. She met Anna on Century Boulevard, and the two girls strolled toward the tiny neighborhood grocery store. It had been there, four blocks from Gordon Brown, for twenty years, with faded, hand-painted letters saying "Century Market" over the front door. Graffiti was scrawled on its walls, and there were wrought-iron bars over the front door and the picture windows. The door bars had flat, black flowers welded to the metal strips to decorate them a little, she guessed. But they still announced to the world that these store owners knew how dangerous the neighborhood could be.

New owners, now—the Choi family. Mashell had been hearing a lot of talk around Gordon Brown. Most residents, Mom and Grandma included, weren't happy with the change. The Chois, you see, were Korean.

"Your family say anything about the new owners?" Mashell asked her friend.

"No. Why?"

"Well, my grandma's all up in arms 'cause she says they got no business makin' money off us. An' then Mom jumps in with her two cents worth—'They don't live 'round here. They don't put nothin' in our community.' They both say the store oughtta be owned by an African-American family. Or Latinos."

"But wasn't that their daughter at Good News Club today?"

"Who? Oh, you mean that new girl? *I* dunno. Maybe they *have* moved here. I never saw her before. She sure was quiet. I hardly noticed her."

"Me, either." They'd reached the store's front door. As Anna pulled it open she said, quietly, "You know, we probably didn't make her feel very welcome."

Both girls entered. The store always seemed dim inside, despite the fluorescent lights overhead. Maybe it was the narrow aisles or the scuffed, gray linoleum on the floor or the crammed shelves. Mashell nearly had to push her way past somebody she knew—a tall, big-waisted older woman with white, curly hair like Grandma's. Her name was Mrs. Ethel Johnson. She lived at Gordon Brown too, and she was best known for being on the residents' committee and arguing a lot at the community meetings.

She was wearing a yellow, short-sleeved smock dress and tennis shoes. Mashell murmured, "Hello, Mrs. Johnson," but Mrs. Johnson was too upset to notice. She stood waving a bunch of bananas and complaining.

"You chargin' way too much for these! The previous owners, they *never* asked this much."

The man behind the counter was obviously either the

new owner or a relative. He was thin, with the same straight, black hair and flat nose Mashell had noticed on Judy Choi. He looked very uncomfortable at the moment. "Sorry, lady," he answered, "but we are having trouble with the shipping company. See? They tell us the bananas didn't grow well this season. They have to charge us a lot more."

"Yeah, right! *Liar!* You just tryin' to *gouge* us!"

The woman flung the bananas on the counter and stalked out of the store. Mashell and Anna exchanged *ooh boy* glances. They weren't the only ones failing to make the Chois feel welcome.

Carlos called Peppy out of the back of Stan's truck, and the dog jumped down immediately. The boy wasn't used to seeing a shiny, new, chain-link training collar around the dog's neck or hearing it chinkle softly. He gripped Peppy's black leather leash firmly and followed Stan and Miss Lindstrom.

The young adults each led a dog. Charlie was calm (at the moment) and Miss Lindstrom walked with another golden retriever named Mike at her side. He was a darker rust than Peppy and not quite as tall or broad chested. Miss Lindstrom had kept him from getting sent to the pound, which made Carlos glad all over every time he saw him. Mike was way too nice a dog to be destroyed.

The three animals were good friends. Thankfully they'd worn off some of their hyper delight at seeing each other before Stan ever let them into his truck. But Carlos knew they'd erupt again when they saw other dogs. And there promised to be lots of them. He could see them in the distance, clustered around a wide-trunked tree.

The class was meeting in the biggest park Carlos had ever seen. They were miles from Watts, in a suburb called Redondo Beach. They were close to the Pacific Ocean; Carlos caught glimpses of water through the trees and houses on the surrounding streets. From this distance, the ocean looked like a silvery-blue, flat sheet reaching a third of the way up the sky. He could smell it, too—the sort of fishy freshness of sea air. There wasn't nearly as much smog here, either.

The grass was green and thick and felt good under his tennis shoes. Lots of bushes and flowers, too. And at least two sets of playground equipment and a huge open area for romping—and training dogs. He *liked* this place.

Peppy seemed to like it, too. He had a doggy grin on his face and his steps were jouncy. He (and the other two) kept making quick stops to sniff things. Carlos had brought along his "go-get-it" ball because he knew his dog would expect a game of fetch in a place like this. After the class was over.

They'd drawn close enough to the crowd of people and

canines for Carlos to see what they were: lanky Dalmatians and curly-haired poodles, a graceful collie, an Alaskan malamute with a curled-up tail, a short-legged beagle, a brawny Rottweiler, a gentle-eyed cocker spaniel. And a teeny white dog that made Carlos laugh because it looked like a mop head with a tiny, black nose. Its little eyes barely showed for the fur hanging in front of them. "What kind is that?" he asked the two adults.

"A Maltese," answered Stan.

A short, thin man stood off from the rest, clutching the leash of a long-legged Doberman pinscher and looking harried. The boy found out why in the next moment. The Doberman caught sight of the three approaching dogs (who were giddy over meeting new friends) and lunged at them, barking in the loudest, snarliest, *nastiest* voice Carlos had ever heard a dog use.

"Stop that right now!" croaked its owner, trying to tow his furious dog backwards. It strained against its leash, and Carlos suddenly felt afraid. *What if it broke loose?* It looked mad enough to kill somebody!

A brown-haired, broad-shouldered man wearing jeans

and a blue T-shirt burst from the crowd, grabbed the Doberman's leash and gave it a series of quick, vicious jerks. "No, no, *no, NO!"* he bellowed.

The dog hopped backwards and stopped struggling, hating the sharp pinches it was getting from its chain-link collar. It drew off its attack and shut up, though it clearly wanted to keep going for Charlie's or Mike's or *Peppy's* throat. Carlos was amazed! That guy got the beast to calm down in just *seconds.*

He was obviously the class trainer. "You see how effective a training collar can be," he said to the crowd. "It's very important that you give a misbehaving dog *rapid, short* jerks of the leash. Okay? Jerk, *release*—instantly. *Don't* pull and hold tight or you'll choke your dog."

The Doberman, realizing it couldn't attack, decided to continue the chewing-out it had started. It pinned a fierce gaze on Charlie and went back to rapid-fire snarls and barks.

Before the trainer could jerk the Doberman's leash again, Charlie answered back. He'd been making friendly grunts and "play bobs" until the Doberman first lunged at him. But now he raised himself to his full, four-legged height, which brought his eyes nearly level with Carlos'!

His voice boomed out like a living foghorn. "*Horf! Row-warf, ROARFF!*" He threw in a snort, stamped his front paws and ended with "*RrrrOAFF!!*"

The Doberman lowered its tail and scuttled behind its master. Everybody whistled and clapped for Charlie. Stan patted his head, looking pleased. "You sure told him!" raved Carlos.

The Doberman's owner was plainly relieved, but embarrassed too. The class trainer chuckled and placed his hand on the man's left shoulder. "Look. You work hard and do everything I tell you and you'll have this dog under control." He raised his voice so the whole class could hear him. "See, our Doberman here is a good example of a *bluffer.* All tough on the face of it. But the first dog that calls his bluff sends him cowering."

He nodded at Charlie. "But then, I'd back down too, if my challenge was being answered by *that* boy."

Everybody laughed, including Stan. Charlie sat panting and looking the most pleased of all.

The class trainer introduced himself as Greg Milton and made it a point to greet the three new dogs, too. He especially liked Peppy. "Look at this handsome guy! He's in fantastic shape. You've taken good care of him." (Carlos couldn't keep from grinning at that.) "I love seeing a full-blooded golden in his prime."

Carlos had been working hard, holding a clipboard and filling out a form attached to it. *"Full-blooded?"* he squawked. "I didn't think he was, man! I always figured he was a mix. See, I live in Watts and I found him in an alley, you know? Nobody'd be dumb enough to dump a purebred golden retriever on the streets, would they?"

He was too shocked to go on writing. Greg gave his head a cynical shake. "You'd be amazed at what some jerks do. They pay eight hundred dollars for a puppy, then when it reaches the hyper, chewing stage they decide they can't stand to have it around. And then they don't bother to train it so it becomes well-behaved. Or find a better home for it. They just drop it off on some street and roar away, with the poor thing chasing their car until it can't see them anymore."

Rage rose up inside Carlos. Somebody must have done that to Peppy! He'd found the pup when he was about six months old, scrawny and filthy and flea-ridden and trembling. The boy could see he'd been living in lonely terror and misery, slowly starving to death. He took him home and babied him. And the boy and dog fell nose over heels in love with each other.

"Oh yeah," continued Greg. "He's purebred. I'd stake my reputation on it. Way to go, rescuing him! I can see how smart he is, and how loyal he is to you. You two could make a pretty awesome team."

He left him to greet some other dogs and owners coming for the class. Carlos hurried through the rest of the form. His writing looked funny because he felt so proud and excited he was shivering. He and Peppy *would* make an awesome team, he just knew it! He could hardly wait for the class to get *rolling*.

Greg owned a German shepherd dog—a female named Roxy—who remained at her master's side constantly unless he told her to do otherwise. She was so well-trained he simply let her leash drag loose behind her, utterly confident she'd never run away. "You're gonna be just like that," Carlos whispered to Peppy, who promptly licked the boy's face.

Greg had all the owners and dogs facing him in a huge circle with him and Roxy in the center. (The thin man and his Doberman were standing well outside the circle, in case the "bluff dog" turned into a real attacker.) "First command," he told the class in a voice that boomed over the swishes of wind and the distant squeals of playing kids. "Sit."

He talked through the process then used Roxy to demonstrate. Peppy stood to Carlos' left, looking as eager to try it as his young master. Carlos practiced the hand signal for sit—left hand raised up, palm in, fingers together.

"Okay, try it," Greg said. "Remember, don't push the rear end down. Use a light jerk of the collar to raise your dog's head, and guide his back hips down with a gentle *touch*. And give him lots of praise when he does it right."

Carlos said Peppy's name so he'd look him in the eye. The boy's heart was thumping. "Sit!" he said firmly, bringing his left hand up for the hand signal. He gently tugged Peppy's leash up and slightly back, hoping the collar wouldn't sting him *too* much. It didn't seem to bother him at all. His head rose. At that moment, Carlos tapped the dog's hips with his left thumb and forefinger. Peppy's back legs bent instantly and he smoothly tucked them into the sitting position. *"Good boy!* You're the *best!"*

Peppy was getting excited. He hopped up with a snort, and Carlos could tell he wanted to *wrestle*. "Later," he promised him with a chuckle.

He made sure he had the dog's eye again. "Sit!"

Plop! Peppy dropped his haunches into the sitting position. "Good *boy! Good boy!* I only had to tell you *once!"*

"Ruh!" breathed Peppy. His young master roughed up the hair between his ears and stole a few looks around the circle. The other dogs needed to hear the command several times before they obeyed. Some of them weren't paying any attention to their masters. Some of them wouldn't bend their back legs. One lady was shoving on her poodle's rump with both hands. "Use your leash!" Greg ordered her. "Raise Queenie's head first!"

The little Maltese kept flopping on its back and waving its front paws at its master, a huge man with long legs and a big stomach. He didn't look like he had the heart to reprimand the little thing. Carlos started to laugh. *Oops! Greg was watching!* The boy walked Peppy forward a few steps then commanded, "Sit."

It was like his golden retriever was a robot dog—he obeyed the first time, every time. "I knew he was smart," murmured Greg. Carlos beamed. Meanwhile, he noticed Mike and Charlie. Mike was doing pretty well, but Stan was having a *terrible* time getting Charlie to bend those massive hips of his. He kept rising up and licking his master's face, which was pretty easy for him since he was as tall as Stan when he stood on his back legs!

"No! I love you too, but *sit!*" Stan kept yelling. He tried to grasp Charlie's front paws and pull them down, lost his footing and wound up on his hands and knees with

Charlie straddling his back. *"Off,* Charlie! You're too big! Charlie, *move—"* His words were cut off as the Great Dane, busily squirming off his master's back, whapped Stan's face with his tail. The dog pulled free with a happy, low-voiced grunt and sprang backwards. He wanted to *play.*

Stan picked himself up, brushing grass clippings and dog saliva off his clothes. "Having a problem?" asked Greg brightly. He raised his voice. "Okay, here's a perfect time to show you how to keep your dog from jumping on you and other people . . . ."

Greg called Charlie to him, sounding excited. The Great Dane roared at him with a look in his eyes that said, *Oh boy, oh boy, oh boy!* Carlos, who'd been snickering the whole time, *really* cut loose now.

The megadog planted his back legs and leaped up, aiming to rest his front paws on Greg's shoulders. And just like *that* Greg bellowed *"NO!!"* The trainer also thrust both hands at him, as though he planned to push him over backwards.

Charlie dropped to a sit, looking shocked. *"Good dog!"* exclaimed Greg, pat-slapping his back. Which made the Great Dane so happy he tried jumping up again.

"NO!!" More hand thrusts. More glowing praise when he sat.

The trainer backed up and called him again. This time Charlie barreled up to him, but stopped and sat when he reached him. Stan was flabbergasted.

"You try it now."

Stan called Charlie's name, wincing as the dog pelted up to him. The front legs rose up, Stan bellowed and thrust in imitation of his teacher—and it *worked!* Stan was so happy he broke into high-pitched laughter.

"Now, let's get him to obey the sit command," said Greg.

Meanwhile, Carlos tried the "no jumping up" technique with Peppy, who was a *master* at nearly knocking people over on their backs. It worked right away, of course. But Carlos almost felt bad. Greg noticed. "What's the matter?" he asked him.

"I kind of *liked* it when he jumped on me!"

* * * * * * * *

They learned the "come" and "stay" commands. Peppy

sat like a rock for twenty seconds, once he understood he wasn't supposed to move. The dog easily learned to "heel" on the leash too, prancing smartly at his young master's left side, head up, chest out, not surging ahead or lagging behind. He followed the boy around perfectly for the "about turn" and instantly sat when Greg called the class to "Halt!" Carlos was tempted to drop the leash the way Greg did for Roxy, but the teacher wouldn't let him. Not yet, anyway.

He was happy to learn that there was a signal he could give Peppy that would let him know it was okay to play. The boy simply needed to drop on all fours and bob his chest down the way Peppy did when he wanted to romp. The golden retriever got the message instantly, and he and Carlos wound up in their usual snorting, laughing mess of arms and legs and fur.

Peppy was the star of the class. Mike had done well too, and Becky made sure he knew it. Charlie had finally gotten the sit command—sort of—but he was *lousy* at heeling, dragging Stan all over the place in spite of his training collar gagging him. But the young man was so thrilled to have gotten the Great Dane over his jumping up that he wasn't too upset. "One thing at a time," he said.

Becky had brought a picnic lunch. They ate at a table under a big tree and tossed balls for the three dogs to catch. But what really made this one of the best days of Carlos' life were the last words Greg said to him before taking off to teach another class. "You need to get an ILP number assigned to Peppy so you can enter him in obedience competitions. See me next class, and I'll explain what it is and give you a form. You two have the makings of a champion team."

Those words kept echoing through Carlos' mind. *Champion team!* Peppy had just brought back his go-get-it ball for another toss from his young master. Carlos scratched his neck and said, "Didn't I tell you? You're the best!"

Mashell and Anna sat on the Hernandez' back steps, watching Maria, Victoria, Loeesha and Rosa while Mama napped. The younger Hernandez girls, aged five and seven, owned only one doll each. Maria's was a plump baby doll, about the size of a real newborn. Victoria had a Barbie with long, wavy black hair and bronze plastic for skin. Mashell insisted the doll looked like Anna. Her friend only shook her head and gave a scoffing laugh.

The little girls were playing house, and the two dolls made for an interesting family. "Maria's baby is gonna have to get a lot thinner if she's supposed to look like her older sister," said Mashell.

Anna chuckled. "Shorter, too. She's taller than Barbie right now, and she's only six weeks old!"

Maria turned and glared at them. "Barbie is the

neighbor."

"Oh," Mashell answered, properly corrected. "But you been talkin' 'bout the three babies. Where are the other two? Do I gotta use my imagination?"

"No." Maria didn't bother to explain further. She simply pointed to Rosa, who was lying sideways on a blanket, sucking orange juice out of a baby bottle.

Mashell laughed. "That's practical. If you ain't got enough baby dolls, use what you *got!* But you still didn't tell me where the third one is."

"Goo, goo, goo!" said Loeesha. That answered that question. She crawled onto Rosa's blanket and cooed the same phrase in her face, which made the *real* baby burst into giggles.

"Go to sleep," Victoria coaxed them. (She always played the mom.) Rosa sat up and flung the bottle away, making it clear she'd do no such thing. Then she grabbed her sister's blouse and tried to pull herself up with a determined grunt.

"No, Rosa! You'll rip it!" gasped Victoria, dropping her

character completely and backing up. Which only made her shirt stretch.

Anna to the rescue. She worked the fabric free from the toddler's pudgy fists then backed up and clapped her hands, beckoning her to come. Rosa stood on her own and scampered to her teen sister. Anna scooped her into her arms. "You old *cheater!* You don't need to pull yourself up on anybody anymore! You're getting bigger all the time. *Aren't* you? Whoo-*eeee!"* She whirled, and Rosa shrieked with laughter.

"Anna, *I'm* the mom," said Victoria, all indignant. Both older girls chuckled over that one.

"*Sorry,* Mrs. Hernandez. Maybe you would like to take your babies for a walk since they don't seem ready for a nap."

"Yeah!" the three little girls chorused.

Ten minutes later the six of them were strolling down the neighborhood sidewalk, with Rosa sitting in the Hernandez' faded, squeaky stroller. (It took some doing to convince Loeesha that she needed to "grow up" so the *real* toddler could ride.) There weren't many people around today. Carlos, who had taken Peppy out to practice, was supposed to be in the front yard. But he was nowhere in sight.

Mashell finally spotted somebody three blocks away, running toward Century Boulevard. She recognized the person and pointed her out to Anna. Judy Choi.

"She in a big hurry. Wonder why."

"You know," Anna began, "I've been feeling really bad about the way we treated her at Good News Club. Like she didn't exist, you know? I bet she thinks we hate her the way everybody else around here hates her family."

"Then how 'bout we make friends *now?*"

"But where'd she go?"

"She prob'ly went to her family's S-T-O-R-E." The girl spelled the word in a vain attempt to keep the younger girls from catching on.

Victoria looked insulted. "That spelled *store.* Why can't *we* go, too?"

Mashell gave Anna a wincing glance. "Who says you can't?"

"I don't got any money," said Anna.

"I got some. Maybe I can get a little treat for all of us."

"Don't spend your money on us!"

"Too late, girlfriend! My mind's made up!"

The little girls cheered, including Rosa, though she couldn't have known what the excitement was about. "I want a candy bar!" Maria exclaimed. The others started listing requests too, until Anna cut them off, sounding just like Mama.

"Girls! Be polite! We'll take whatever Mashell decides to get, and thank her for it!"

"Won't be much! I only got a quarter. Maybe I can get us a little bag of candy."

They hurried along, as fast as the stroller's wobbly wheels would let them. There was no sign of Judy when they entered the store. Mashell and Anna let the little girls study the candy while they spoke to the man behind the counter. (He was the one who'd been chewed out by Mrs. Johnson.)

"Are you Judy's dad?" began Anna.

He nodded. Mashell thought he looked on edge, like he expected Anna to start yelling at him or insulting his daughter. "She visited our Good News Club the other day, and we didn't really say much to her then. We didn't mean to ignore her. It just happened. But we wanna be friends.

Is she around?"

Mr. Choi looked surprised. Taken aback. "Yeah, yeah," he stammered. "She's in the storeroom helping her mother." He called his daughter's name over his shoulder. Judy came out from behind a curtain and froze at the sight of the girls. Anna and Mashell promptly introduced themselves and the younger girls. And apologized for not doing it sooner.

Judy didn't say much except to murmur, "That's okay." She didn't smile, either. Was she shy? Or was she having a hard time believing they actually wanted to be friends?

Just as Mashell was feeling really awkward, they were all distracted by young voices, arguing. "I want the chocolate stars!"

"You can't have them! There isn't enough to go around!"

"Yes, there *is!* I counted 'em! Ten! One, two, three—"

"But that means we'll all only get one, and we can't have two because there isn't enough. There'd be a bunch left over that nobody could eat, 'cause it wouldn't be fair. *I've* learned how to add!"

"Anna!"

The young teen hurried to cut Maria and Victoria's argument short. As it turned out, chocolate stars weren't an option anyway, because they cost too much. "Looks like we don't got many choices," sighed Mashell. "Not if we want somethin' that's got enough for all of us."

"How much money do you have?" asked Mr. Choi.

"Twenty-five cents."

He glanced at the tiny green sticker on the bag. "Thirty-five. Oh, close enough, close enough. You came here to be nice to my daughter. Call it okay."

Anna made sure everybody thanked him. He nodded and smiled. Victoria didn't seem satisfied, though. She tapped Anna's shoulder then whispered urgently, "But what about the *extras?"*

Mashell grinned. "We'll take care of 'em! There's one for Mr. and Mrs. Choi, and *Judy.*" She pulled the cardboard top off the cellophane bag and held it out to the girl. Judy took a star and smiled for the first time. Mr. Choi took his with a nod and shouted for his wife so she could get hers. She was short like her husband, but thicker at the waist, and when he told her why he'd called her from her work she looked at him like he was crazy.

Mashell let Victoria explain the great importance of keeping all things even, and the lady broke into a wide grin. “Okay, okay. Fair is fair!” She took her candy piece and went back behind the curtain, chuckling.

They all ate their stars. But they still had a problem. “There’s one left!” said Maria, looking hungry.

Mashell caught Anna’s eye. “Let’s let Judy have it. We wanna be extra nice to her ’cause we weren’t so great at it last week.”

Judy looked like she was about to cry and waved the candy away. “It’s okay, really. Thanks for wanting to be my friends, but—”

She ducked her head and lost the battle against her tears. A tiny sob escaped her and she whispered, “Excuse me,” then hurried to the other room.

The girls stood in an awkward silence broken only by the hum of refrigerator fans. They heard Judy’s mom scolding her and telling her to go back out to her visitors. The girl only cried harder and refused, though Mashell couldn't make out her words as she told her mom why.

Mr. Choi shook his head, and he looked like he carried an invisible weight on his back. "Please forgive my daughter. She's very upset. I don't blame her."

Mashell had to ask. "Over what?"

He shook his head again. "You're the first people who have been kind to us. And then there's—" The man muttered something about the girls being too young.

Mashell wasn't going to go until she understood what he was talking about. "There's *what?*"

"Where do you live?" he asked Victoria, who was only too happy to tell him.

Fine! thought Mashell. *Change the subject.*

Judy suddenly stepped from behind the curtain and beckoned to Anna and Mashell. Her eyes were red, and now they had anger in them. "I'll show you," she said quietly. Her dad caught her eye and nodded and made clear with a gesture to Anna that he'd watch Rosa.

The older girls quietly followed Judy past the curtain. Mrs. Choi was sitting at a card table surrounded on three sides by stacks of boxes. She rapidly punched numbers into a calculator from piles of receipts scattered across the table. A small television on a stand in front of her filled the little room with a murmur of music and talk. The room was full of scents too— cardboard and soap, and whiffs of mint and chocolate.

Mashell set the plastic bag with the last star in it on the table without saying a word, and Mrs. Choi was too absorbed doing math to notice. Good. She'd find it later.

Judy opened the door in the far wall, and outside light streamed in. They followed her out, then around to the building's side wall—

And Mashell immediately knew what her new friend was so bothered about. Someone had spray-painted giant words on the wall: "Clear out, Koreans, if you want to live." There were other words too, in different colors, probably sprayed by other people. Words that agreed with the original message. And words that were ugly to read. She saw now why Mr. Choi had been hesitant to explain.

"*Man,* that's gross!" she blurted out. "What's the matter with these people?"

Judy was crying again. "I've been getting called names

at school. Coming home today, some guy yelled that he was going to beat me up! I got so scared I ran all the way here!"

"I saw you," put in Mashell quietly.

"I wish my parents had never bought this store!" Her voice took on a bitter edge. "Then Dad says he's getting all kinds of complaints because we make money off this neighborhood, but we don't *live* here, so he moves us into an apartment in Watts! A lot of good it did! Now they want to hurt us! Or *kill* us! *Why?* What did we ever do to anybody?"

"It doesn't make sense," said Anna.

Judy's fury was growing. "Oh yes it does! Can't you read? It's because we're *Korean!* They don't like *us* in their neighborhood!"

Mashell was getting angry too. "Mom an' Grandma an' everybody I know is always talkin' 'bout how bad we African-Americans and Hispanics is treated. An' then we turn around an' treat somebody from *another* race like this!"

"It doesn't make sense," repeated Anna. "If we've been treated wrong because of our race, then we should be extra nice to others, because we know how much it hurts to have people look down on us just because of our skin color."

Mashell scanned the message again, and it made her shudder. "Humans don't work that way, girlfriend. They too stubborn. Too stuck on what *they* want. Once they start hatin', they don't seem to quit."

She wished there was something she could do to change that. Some way she could fight the hate around her. And her thoughts turned into a prayer. *Lord Jesus, will You show me what to do?*

Carlos decided to give Peppy a good run before he started practicing his training. The dog would do even better once he wore away some of the energy he always had so much of. So the two of them left the front yard and romped down the block.

"Hey, I got an even better idea, dog," said Carlos in a voice made shaky from running. "Let's go to the park. That way, you'll be more used to the noise and stuff when we go back to Redondo Beach."

He let Peppy gallop until he needed a rest himself. They were only a couple blocks from the neighborhood park; they could afford to walk the rest of the way.

Carlos suddenly remembered he had forgotten to tell Peppy to heel. But he was doing it perfectly anyway. The boy stopped, gave the command and they went on exactly the same. But now it was official.

Peppy already knew he had to sit the instant his young master stopped walking. "Good boy!"

The boy ran a little ways with Peppy cantering happily beside him, snorting and chuffing. He slowed to a walk and gave the sit command and its hand signal. The retriever didn't respond. He'd probably forgotten the word. Carlos said it again, gave the leash a gentle tug and tapped his dog's back hips . . . and saw a look enter the dog's eyes as if he was thinking, *Oh, yeah! That!* He instantly tucked his back legs under. "Good *boy!"*

He walked him again. "Sit!" Plop! *"Good boy!"* They did it three more times, perfectly. Carlos was getting more excited each time they practiced. This was fun! They *were* a champion team! Peppy was picking up the boy's attitude and seemed to be relishing each command as much as his young master did.

Carlos planted himself in front of the dog and held his flat hand, palm out, in front of Peppy's nose. "Stay!"

He counted out ten seconds, then rotated himself so that he was standing beside his dog. Ten more seconds. Carlos decided to go for twenty. But a lady with strands of gray in her black hair, and a very round stomach, passed by on the nearby sidewalk. A little dog led her on a pink leash. It barked a greeting. Peppy answered and sprang forward two steps.

"No!"

Peppy whirled and stared at his master in surprise, then returned to the sit position, looking a little embarrassed. To the boy's irritation, the middle-aged woman stood nearby with her dog yapping (it was a fuzzy little thing—a mix of poodle and terrier and who knew what else). "See, Kipsy, what a good dog that is? I'd like *you* to do that. So you just watch, now."

Peppy kept wanting to squirm toward the little thing, and Carlos had to keep ordering him to stay. Kipsy scampered in close, dragging the lady by her leash. She wanted to meet the bigger dog, and no amount of her mistress' scolding was going to stop her. The woman finally towed her backwards and picked her up.

"Okay," the boy said, releasing Peppy after twenty seconds and trying not to sound irritated. *Ma'am, get a clue! We're trying to practice here!*

"You sure got a handsome thing there. You trainin'

'im?" the lady asked.

"Yeah. For competition." *What does it look like I'm doing?*

"That so. Tell me about it."

Carlos wanted to tell her he needed to get on with Peppy's work, but he knew that wouldn't be polite. So as briefly as he could he described Greg's class, and the woman said she and Kipsy might want to come next week. Then she nodded at the retriever. "Show me what he can do."

The boy grinned in spite of himself. Suddenly Kipsy wriggled from her mistress' grasp and bounded around Peppy, who leaped after her. They were in serious danger of tangling their leashes! The lady quickly grabbed her little dog (it was the only way she could get her away!), then Carlos called Peppy's name so he'd look at him. "Peppy, sit!"

He did, of course. Carlos glowed with pride. He demonstrated heel and stay. This time the dog sat as still as a rock with his master in front of him for twenty seconds, then alongside him for the same. "Ain't that somethin'," the lady murmured. "That's real good!"

She wanted the boy to show her how to get *Kipsy* to do it. But that was going too far! He was squirming to go on with Peppy's practice, and besides, he wasn't sure he could teach a stubborn dog like hers! He grabbed the first excuse he could think of. "Um, you really shouldn't try this stuff without a training collar on her . . . ."

Then she wanted to know what a training collar was! *Oh brother!* He explained it as quickly as he could then looked desperately for another excuse—and saw it off in the distance in the form of a friend.

Mashell was wandering through the park, looking preoccupied with something. He called out to her, then excused himself from the woman. He made sure he was out of earshot before he muttered, "Dog, from now on we practice in our own yard!"

"What's up?" his friend asked as he and Peppy neared her.

He quickly told her. "What a *brat* that dog Kipsy was! She didn't do anything the lady wanted her to! She had a total mind of her own. She was gonna do what *she* was gonna do!"

"Like people," mumbled Mashell.

He gave her a puzzled look and she described the new graffiti on Century Market and Judy's reaction to it. He shook his head in sympathy. "That's awful, man! The Chois haven't done anything wrong. Why do people *do* stuff like that, you know? I trained Peppy not to jump up on anybody. Too bad you can't train people to quit hating each other!"

Mashell's thought-filled eyes suddenly brightened. "Say that again."

"Too bad you can't train people the way you can train dogs."

"Who *says* you can't?"

He stopped walking. Peppy, at heel, instantly sat. "I'll have to think about it."

"*We'll* think about it, my friend! I think we on to somethin' here! Now, show me what you've trained Peppy to do. And *not* to do."

He sighed and scratched his dog's back. It looked like their private practice would have to wait until later.

* * * * * * * *

Mashell realized she and Carlos couldn't change the

world by themselves; they'd need the help of their friends. They enlisted Anna and Felipe, and the four of them (five with Peppy) went around to all the Good News Club kids (including Judy at the store). They told them to meet in the park tomorrow afternoon after school. "What for?" they all wanted to know.

"People training," Mashell told them, and smiled when they asked what *that* was.

"You just gonna have to wait an' find out."

She found it hard to concentrate during school. Except when she had to write a one-page report on something she'd read recently that *wasn't* a book. She poured out *two* pages, telling her teacher what she thought of the words she'd read on the wall of Century Market. She got a "B" on it. The teacher said that graffiti-reading wasn't exactly what he had in mind for the assignment (he'd expected something from a magazine or a comic book). But he agreed with her feelings.

The Good News Club kids from Fern Street Elementary wound up walking to the park together. Anna, in junior high, met them there. Carlos had gone home to get Peppy, who was key to this whole thing. "Take your time getting there," he'd told her, "'cause I'm gonna put Peppy through his *dog*-training practice first."

So they waited under a tree that had a gnarled, stocky trunk and dark green leaves so smooth and shiny they looked like they were waxed. "Does this have something to do with the graffiti on my store?" Judy asked Mashell.

She grinned mysteriously.

"I'm hungry," complained nine-year-old Nathan.

The cluster of ten kids was getting ready to break apart for home when Anna spotted her brother loping toward them with Peppy trotting at his side. "About *time* you got here!" yelled Bronce.

Carlos didn't answer until he reached the group. "Sorry I'm late. But Peppy and me, we gotta keep practicing so we can be *champions.*"

Of course the Good News Club kids wanted to know of *what?* He explained, which gave Mashell a perfect lead-in. "See, he trainin' his dog to be good an' win competitions an' things. An' not do *bad* things. Show 'em, Carlos!"

He did. The dog obeyed the commands perfectly. The kids were impressed, especially when he sat absolutely still for one whole minute. Carlos even pulled an old tennis ball, more gray than yellow, from his pocket and tossed it. The dog stared at it and quivered, but he didn't so much as shift a paw—until his young master said, "Okay, *go get it!*" Then Peppy flung himself at it as fast as his legs could move.

The kids cheered, and Peppy scampered among them, catching pats and strokes in passing, showing off his prize as if it was pure gold. "I just tried that today," Carlos explained proudly. "He's learning to stay no matter what."

He pursed his lips. "He's been doing so well with 'come' when he's on the leash . . . ." His voice trailed away and Mashell watched him grapple with a decision. "Greg said not to try this without having our dogs on a leash yet. But he's doing so good . . . I'm gonna try it! Peppy, *come.*"

The dog instantly turned and looked at his master. But Bronce was giving him a *heavenly* chest rub. He stayed put.

"COME!"

No response. "Quit petting him," ordered Carlos quietly. Bronce obeyed, and backed up. Peppy started to inch toward him while everyone watched, hardly breathing, to see what Carlos would do.

"NO!"

The dog stopped moving and looked worried, as though he wasn't sure what to do. Carlos looked worried too. "I shouldn't have tried this," he muttered. "I think I'm confusing him." Mashell watched him try to think his way out of the situation. Suddenly he smiled and his voice went bright and cheerful. "Peppy, *come.*"

The retriever seemed to grin. He leaped forward and loped to Carlos, who looked deeply relieved and raved that he was the *best.* The kids clapped.

Mashell jumped on the opportunity. "If Carlos can train Peppy to quit jumpin' on people an' come when he called an' stuff, why couldn't *we* train the kids an' even the grownups around here to quit hatin' each other? Why couldn't we train 'em to do nice things instead of all this *mean* stuff like taggin' the Choi's store with foul words, just 'cause they Korean?" She glanced at Judy, who looked like she was fighting away tears.

Nobody said anything for a moment. She was pleased to see them thinking about it and not making fun of her idea. She expected the question Felipe asked. *"How?"*

Carlos took the cue. "Well, like with Peppy, I make it

uncomfortable for him if he does something wrong—like yelling "No!" at him or jerking his leash so his training collar pinches his neck. And I make it nice for him when he obeys my commands. You know, petting him and making a big deal out of him."

"What we supposed to do," cut in Bronce. "Make everybody in Watts wear leashes an' chain collars like Peppy's got? An' when we see somebody hatin' somebody else we run up and yank their collars?"

Everybody laughed, especially Mashell. "We can't *punish* nobody, that's for sure! Especially adults. *Hoo!* Great way to get ourselves *shot!* But I was thinkin' we could do somethin' nice to somebody when we see 'em bein' kind . . . ."

"Like our teachers at Good News Club?" said Anna. "They let us take a prize out of the prize bag if we haven't gotten any checks."

They all knew what she was talking about. The club teachers would put checks beside their names on the attendance sheets, for talking without permission or bothering kids around them or getting out of their chairs without asking or hitting somebody or name-calling . . . .

"Give people *yo-yos?"* asked Nathan.

Mashell shrugged. "Make 'em feel good somehow. Not *yo-yos,* but *somethin'."* She was thinking hard. What was it about the word "command" that struck a chord with her? She turned to Carlos. "Say, what you mean by a command? Is that when you tell Peppy to *sit* an' all that?"

"Yeah. It's anything I want him to do—sit, heel, come, stay. I'll learn more next class."

She grinned with triumph as she remembered where she'd used that word a lot this week. "John fifteen, seventeen," she began. The others instantly joined her. And this time they all recited the verse the way Mrs. Peterson had taught them. "'This is my command. Love each other.' John fifteen, seventeen."

Mashell was getting excited. She'd just gotten a *fabulous* idea, and somehow she knew that this was the answer to her prayer. "Look, what if we was *sneaky* about all this? We could write that verse on one side of a bunch of pieces of paper. And on the other side we could say 'You obeyed God's command' an' then sign some name to it that we wanna call ourselves. Then we could *slip* them at people, you know? Give 'em to 'em when they ain't lookin', so they'll just look down and find 'em, an' not know who did it."

She saw grins and heard quick chuckles. "That sounds fun," said Felipe.

Bronce went a step further. "Couldn't we leave notes tellin' somebody bein' a jerk that they *ain't* obeyin' God's command?"

"I guess we could," said Carlos in an I'm-not-so-sure-about-this voice. "If we were careful not to get caught."

"I'd be careful. They'd never know what hit 'em!" Bronce declared.

They were getting more excited. But then Nathan cooled them off a little by pointing out a practical problem. "What if the wind blows the paper away before they read it?"

Now they all stopped to think. "Tape?" suggested Felipe.

Mashell shook her head. "We couldn't get away fast enough. We'd have to hang around stickin' it on."

"Sticky notes!" said Anna.

The kids who knew what they were laughed or said,

"Yeah!" Those that didn't looked confused.

She quickly explained. "They're those little pieces of paper that have sticky stuff on the back. You just pull them off their stack and stick them where you want them."

"They're *perfect!*" gloated Mashell. "Cheap, too. I seen 'em at the dollar store. If we all pitched in we could buy enough to leave a note to everybody in L.A.!" She was exaggerating of course. "So what we gonna call ourselves?"

"But we're already the Good News Club!" protested Juan.

"I know, but this is a little somethin' more. An' what if we decide to let other kids join us, like at school, that *ain't* in the Good News Club?"

Her logic was good, and she could tell they knew it. They all poured themselves into thinking again. Bronce was first to volunteer a name. "How 'bout the Secret Note Givers?"

"Nah!" they chorused.

Other ideas popped out of the young heads gathered under the tree. "The Secret Messengers!" "The Sneak Police!"

Mashell waved at the group to be quiet. "Let's quit with

this *secret* an' *sneaky* stuff! If we call ourselves that, everybody'll *know* we a secret!"

Judy spoke up for the first time. "I have one. How about the Hate Fighters?"

Everybody kept silent, letting it sink in. "Yeah," began Mashell slowly. Then her enthusiasm grew. "Yeah! The Hate Fighters! I *like* that!"

They all agreed. Judy really smiled for the first time since she'd joined the Good News Club. "You're the first friends I've had since I moved here," she said. "You guys are great!"

Mashell caught Anna's eye and grinned. So far, the Hate Fighters were practicing what they were about to preach.

They decided to let Anna, Mashell, Bronce and Judy write the messages—their handwriting looked closest to adult. "Ain't no good havin' everybody figure out we kids. Where's the secret in that?" Mashell had pointed out. So they pooled their dimes and quarters and paraded to the dollar store to buy the notes. Yellow for pointing out kindness and blue for warning those who disobey God's command.

Carlos and Felipe spent about half an hour that evening sitting on Anna's bed and watching the girls handwrite the messages. Mashell had even bought different colored pens, for variety. "What if the person who gets that doesn't *care?*" asked Felipe as he watched her write a warning message in neon green.

She shrugged. "Ain't no good worryin' 'bout what

somebody thinks of these. Our job is to get the message *out.* It's like we yankin' their chains. It may make 'em sting a *little,* anyway."

The boys grew bored with the process and went to play in the backyard. The next morning, they helped the writers give out four stacks of the little, square notes, one hundred sheets per stack, to each Hate Fighter. Two hundred compliments and two hundred warnings.

School wouldn't start for twenty minutes. The Hate Fighters split into pairs and wandered around the crowded, fenced-in playground, alert for any acts of kindness or meanness or prejudice. Carlos dropped his notes in his jeans pocket and went with Felipe, of course. He felt like Batman with Robin at his side.

One of their classmates was leaning against a tan brick wall, holding his school books and looking cranky. Two first-grade boys pounded past him with the bouncy laughs of kids running on concrete. Suddenly the fifth grader bellowed, caught the second boy by his shirt, and yelled, "You ran over my *toe,* you brain-dead little *klutz!*"

His name was Doug, and if he was in a bad mood, *watch*

out. "Let go!" wailed the younger boy. The fifth grader shoved him hard, then stepped forward to push the whimpering kid again.

Felipe strolled up to his right side, blocking him in a subtle sort of way. "Hey, Doug, is your toe okay?"

"What do *you* care?"

"I hate it when somebody steps on my toe. Why shouldn't I care about *yours?"* While Felipe talked, Carlos reached Doug's left side and didn't waste a second. Neither did the first grader, who wisely bolted away. Five minutes later Doug looked down at his math book and saw a small square of blue stuck to it. "Batman and Robin" watched him frown as he read it. Then he crumpled it and threw it away. But he didn't push any more first graders during this playtime, anyway.

They saw a third-grade girl run to her friend who'd tripped and turned her ankle. She comforted her and helped her to her feet. And two minutes later she was shocked (and pleased) to find a yellow square stuck to her sweater that told her she'd obeyed God's command to love.

Felipe grinned at Carlos and spoke in a low voice.

"Didn't I tell you this would be fun?"

The bell rang. The school kids lined up with their classes against their assigned walls. The Hate Fighters were already having an effect. Clusters of fifth graders were chattering about the little papers that mysteriously showed up on books and clothes and *backs,* even. They wondered who the Hate Fighters were. (Doug didn't say a word.) Carlos tried to look as innocent as possible. *He'd* never tell.

They did the same thing every recess. After school they met briefly to agree which routes to take and then *hit the streets*. Yellow and blue squares appeared on windows and doors, car windshields, purses, shopping bags. Whenever a person was kind or mean. Gracious or impatient. Polite or rude. Open-hearted or prejudiced.

"I can't do this for too long. I gotta practice with Peppy," Carlos told Felipe with regret. He knew it was vital to work with his dog, and he *loved* it. But this Hate Fighter stuff was also a blast!

They were prowling along Century Boulevard, listening and looking hard. There! An African-American teenager was telling her Hispanic girlfriend she liked her hairstyle. Carlos ambled by the bus bench they were sitting on, pretended to drop a book and stuck a yellow note to her purse. As the two boys rounded the next corner, he heard her let out a yelp. "Hey! What in the *world?* Girl, did you put this on here?"

They snickered. They'd been hearing that kind of thing all day. But then Carlos saw something near the 103rd Street train station that made him stop cold. A boy Carlos recognized from the other fifth-grade class at Fern Street Elementary was standing near the tracks. The boy picked up a small white stone (the train track borders were lined with them) and hurled it at a passing car. He was surrounded by friends, and they all started throwing rocks. And yelling nasty things about the races of the people who drove past them.

Carlos and Felipe exchanged anxious glances. This could be *tricky.* They didn't want to get *beaten up* or anything. Felipe nodded at the street light. *Yeah!* It was red, and the rock throwers would have to wait to cross the street. The two Hate Fighters caught up with them, and without being obvious about it, hovered alongside them as they all waited for the "walk" signal.

Carlos reached in his right pocket, pulled a blue square free and waited with a thumping heart for the exact right moment to . . . . *Okay! The light changed!* The rock throwers, totally ignoring their walking companions, surged ahead. Carlos quickly slapped the note on the first thrower's book bag then slowed down and scanned the scene with his eyes. Nobody noticed, thank goodness! Not yet, anyway. He and Felipe didn't hang around waiting for them to find it and figure out who left it.

They turned onto Century Boulevard. Two men were sitting inside a restaurant, arguing. Their angry voices carried through the open, screened-in window they sat beside. Felipe ran to it and slapped a blue slip on the screen. One of the shouters stopped in mid-sentence to read this little note somebody had just put in his face. The boys scooted to the nearest alley and peeked out to see him come out the door, pull the note off the screen and read both sides.

He scratched his head and looked around (which made the boys duck), then pocketed the slip of paper and walked slowly back inside. He seemed moved by what he read. And the argument didn't start up again.

Carlos and Felipe slapped hands. They passed a discount T-shirt shop and Mashell's favorite thrift store where everything cost a dollar or less. They were coming up on the Chois' Century Market. Mr. Choi was standing on the edge of the sidewalk beside a wooden stand full of fresh lettuce and cabbage heads, tomatoes and onions and potatoes. A large woman faced him, wearing a loose-fitting blouse with lavender stripes and matching slacks that were too short, leaving a gap between her pants and tennis shoes. She was talking a mile a minute and sounding furious.

"Rippin' us off! That's what you doin'!" she was saying. "I ain't payin' that much for tomatoes an' I *ain't* shoppin' here no more. I'm gonna give my business to my *own kind* if I gotta ride the bus all *day* to get my groceries!"

She stomped away in a huff. Felipe was about to slap a blue note on her purse when Carlos stopped him. "Hold it!" he hissed. "Somebody beat us to it!"

A blue square was stuck crookedly to the vinyl handles. The lady moved to adjust them higher on her shoulders and her hand ran against it. She pulled it free and stared at it. Her scowl deepened and her voice grew louder. She stalked back to the store and waved the slip in poor Mr. Choi's face.

"Did *you* put this on my purse?"

He shook his head and looked completely surprised when he read it. "No, ma'am! I never—"

She didn't let him finish and she obviously didn't believe him. "I ain't takin' high prices *and* insults! What right do you got tellin' *me* what God commands? You just wait 'til my friends hear about this! You oughtta be *ashamed* of yourself!"

Mr. Choi looked more upset the more she talked. "Please ma'am, I tell you, I didn't write that. Please, you can check my handwriting . . . ."

Carlos squirmed. Somebody should *do* something. This lady was accusing Mr. Choi of something he didn't do. He thought about speaking up. Never *mind* that the Hate Fighters were supposed to be kept secret. But someone beat him to it. Judy burst through the doorway with Mashell and Anna close behind her. "*I* put the note on your purse!" she declared.

The woman's face turned red. "Well, somebody needs to teach you *respect!*" Then she waved her finger at Mr. Choi. "So help me, I'll see you put out of business!"

She stormed away, and Judy rushed back inside the store. Mr. Choi, too agitated to notice the four kids standing around fidgeting, hurried after her. They could easily hear him scolding his daughter, and they could tell she was crying.

Mashell edged closer to Carlos. "That's Mrs. Johnson. She lives near me. The thing is, if anybody *deserves* a blue slip right now, it's *her*." She shook her head. "Wonder why some people get so mad when you tell 'em the truth."

"'Cause they don't like seeing ugly stuff in themselves," said Carlos in a low voice. "They wanna believe they're perfect, you know?"

Felipe was still holding the blue slip he'd intended to stick on Mrs. Johnson's purse. He looked at it and grimaced. Carlos could tell what he was thinking, and said it out loud. "These notes, they were a good idea. Who knew they'd backfire like this?"

Mashell nodded. "For all we know, we just drove the Chois outta business."

They wondered if they should keep giving out the messages. But everybody at school was talking about them, even the teachers. About what a good idea they were. The playground *did* seem friendlier the next morning. "Besides, kids are expectin' to get a yellow slip when they do somethin' nice. We the Hate Fighters. We can't let 'em down," insisted Mashell.

Carlos nodded. "And I don't think they like getting blue slips, 'cause nobody's being mean." He broke into a grin. "You know, I think we really are people-training!"

Judy made a disgusted face. "I wish Mrs. Johnson had reacted the same way."

"I think it's easier to train kids than adults," said Felipe.

The group spread out, leaving notes as they went. By the end of the day Carlos had far fewer yellow than blue squares left and found the same was true for the others. This Hate Fighter thing was working!

What was amazing was that no one had gotten caught leaving the slips. Yet.

* * * * * * * * *

Mashell had to laugh at the look on Mrs. Peterson's face when all thirty kids at Good News Club recited John fifteen, seventeen perfectly—before she even had time to hold up the memory verse poster. This was one Bible verse they *knew.*

When Miss Lindstrom led them in singing their favorite songs—"Hallelujah Ballad" and "Just Turn Around" and "Jesus Is Caring for You"—they didn't pour out their usual gripes ("No fair!" "You never pick me!") when she picked kids to hold up the words.

When Juan gave up his chair so Judy could sit down, and when at least five kids scrambled to pick up Nathan's dropped pencil for him, and when the opposing teams clapped when their teammates *and* their competitors got the right answer, the three teachers looked pleased but suspicious. Mrs. Joyce gave them her standard, arms-folded glare, though her eyes were sparkling. "All right you guys! What you up to? Tryin' to win extra prizes?"

Everybody snickered but nobody answered.

The best was yet to come. Mrs. Peterson, as she did at every club, had the kids bow their heads for prayer. Then she asked if anybody wanted to become a Christian. "Would you like to pray to God's Son? Would you like Him to make you His child?" And to Mashell's surprise, Judy Choi raised her hand. *I thought she already was a Christian! She goes to church! She knows Bible verses. . . . Maybe she ain't saved yet 'cause she never asked!*

Judy and two other kids left their chairs and followed Mrs. Joyce into the next room. Mashell knew they'd spend several minutes talking to the lady as she made sure they understood what Jesus did for them. She could just hear the teacher asking, "Why did the Lord let those Roman soldiers nail Him by His wrists to that crossbeam of wood?"

If Judy knew, she'd answer, "Because He wanted to take our—my—sins away." The lady would nod, and coax her to explain more. Maybe Judy would say, "He knew I couldn't get into Heaven by myself because I'm not perfect. I've done bad things, and God can't let anybody that's sinned into Heaven because it's perfect, like Him."

Mashell pictured Mrs. Joyce nodding and asking the other kids what they thought. If they were confused, she'd make it clear. "Jesus was perfect too. He never sinned even once. But He let Himself be killed the way they killed criminals two thousand years ago—by gettin' nailed to a cross and hangin' there for *hours* until He died. My, *my* how He must've suffered!"

She'd shake her head in amazement. "An' as if that wasn't hard enough, somehow God put all the wrong things everybody in this world has ever done and ever *would* do on Him. Jesus let Himself get punished for all the murders and mean words, for all the disobedience, for all the stealin' and cheatin' and lyin', for all the hate . . . for every sin us humans do. An' because *He* got punished in our place, He can save us from those sins. He rescues us, like. He can keep us from bein' punished forever in that awful place where the devil is. We just gotta ask Him to."

Once she was sure the three kids understood what Jesus' death was all about, she'd remind them that He wasn't dead anymore. "He came back to *life* again, three days later! God the Father raised Him up! Hallelujah!" Then she'd ask, "What do you want Jesus to do for you?"

And Mashell smiled as she imagined Judy saying, "I want Him to save me from my sins. I want Him to take them away. I want Him to make me His daughter and let me into Heaven someday." And Mrs. Joyce would listen as Judy asked the Lord to do those things for her.

So when Judy and the other two kids walked back into the main meeting room with joy in their eyes and slightly embarrassed grins on their faces, Mashell wasn't at all surprised. She gave Judy's hand a squeeze that said, *I'm happy for you, girlfriend!*

When club was over, the three women gave out their usual hugs and sent the kids home. Little did they know as they talked and picked up their teaching supplies that most of the club was gathered under the windows, silently shushing each other so they could hear their teachers' reactions when they found little yellow message squares stuck to their carrying bags.

* * * * * * * *

The Doberman seemed much calmer this time. His owner had obviously worked with him. Carlos walked toward the circle of dogs with Peppy heeling by his left side. Stan and Miss Lindstrom followed him. Mike was prancing nicely beside Becky, and even Charlie was doing it mostly right. He only started to tug against the leash—chuffing and choking—as he and Stan reached the other animals.

His master got him to sit eventually, which was more than could be said for some of the other dogs. Most of the owners were cramming in a last-minute practice before the class started. Carlos saw there was going to be a big difference between the people who'd practiced during the week and those who hadn't. Charlie, for example, didn't always obey because he didn't always *want* to. But he knew what to *do* anyway, because Stan had been working with him. Some people's dogs, on the other hand, looked as confused by the commands as they had during the first class.

Then Carlos heard sharp yaps. He recognized the sound and the lady dressed in black leggings and a T-shirt who hurried toward them. She was getting dragged by a fuzzy little dog on a pink leash. *Kipsy!* The boy wondered how she'd do.

He grinned at Peppy. There was no question in his mind how *he'd* do. They'd worked hard. They'd practiced twice every day for twice as long as Greg had told them to. They couldn't help it. They both loved it! The boy couldn't imagine feeling any other way. But then, he couldn't imagine owning any other dog but Peppy. He couldn't wait for the first competition. They'd win for sure.

Greg officially started the class by reviewing last week's commands. Their assignment had been to stretch the dogs' stay time to one minute with the owner standing in front and one minute standing alongside. Peppy was up to three minutes each way. Carlos had been sorely tempted to take off his leash, but the near disaster in the park kept him from getting cocky. His dog was doing wonderfully. Why ruin a good thing by pushing him too fast?

Peppy went through all the commands like a champion, and Carlos felt another rush of excited pride when Greg praised him for it. Then Greg took the class on to new things. He added direction changes—right and left turns—to the heel, to go along with the about turn, in which the owners and their dogs turned all the way around and walked back in the opposite direction.

Well, most of them did. Kipsy pulled her mistress every which way. And the tiny Maltese kept wanting to cross in front of its huge owner, who tried to gently push it into place alongside him with his foot. Which made the little thing think he wanted to play. It would dance on its hind legs then scamper around the man, wrapping his ankles with its leash.

Charlie, eager to say hello to a Dalmatian, crossed in front of Stan, too. The young man chose just that moment to turn his head toward Becky. "Hey, Mike seems to be do-*ING—*" He never finished the sentence. His legs hit the thigh-high wall across his path that Charlie had become. He might have been saved if the Great Dane hadn't flinched sideways. But running into a solid object, then having it shift suddenly away, set him doing a desperate dance, knees high and arms flailing! Charlie finished him off by breaking into a run toward the Dalmatian. Stan, staunchly holding his leash, was jerked face first onto the grass.

Which caught Charlie's interest even more than the other dog. He gave a long, low grunt that meant, *Oh, good!*

Playtime! Then he bounded back to his master and circled him like the Maltese was doing—but on a much grander scale.

Stan sat up and bellowed, *"H-E-E-E-E-L!"* Charlie bounced in close to lick his face, which brought him to his feet again in a hurry.

"Keep practicing," was all Greg said.

He taught them to break into a run with the dogs keeping pace by their owners' sides—in theory anyway. They did the same thing walking slowly. The point was, the dogs were to stay alongside their owners' left legs no matter what speed they went. Greg called out the speeds—normal, slow and fast. Charlie, already excited, was thrilled to run, but he didn't want to go slowly at all. Stan nearly lost his footing again. Kipsy went at her *own* pace, thank you very much.

Peppy did it perfectly.

Greg taught them the "down" command by demonstrating with Roxy while he described it. "Have your dog sit by your left side. Kneel beside her (Carlos understood he was talking about both males and females, but was using "her" because of Roxy). Now, reach over her back with your left arm, take hold of her left front leg, and *gently* grab her right leg with your right hand."

He showed them what he meant. He looked like he was hugging his dog from behind. "Okay. Give the command, *'Down.'* Lift the front legs off the ground just a *little* and ease them forward until your dog is lying stretched out on her stomach. Then heap on the praise."

He released Roxy from the position, gave her the sit command, then said, "Down." She dropped flat and looked calmly at her master, waiting for the next command. *(Talk about a robot dog!)* Greg patted her head. "Try it," he told the class.

Even Carlos had trouble getting Peppy to do this command at first. The retriever kept assuming he wanted to wrestle and squirmed and twisted until he could lick the boy's face. "No!" Carlos kept saying between giggles.

Greg raised one eyebrow, but he looked amused. "That's what you get for playing so rough. Pull his front legs down *quickly*, before he has time to really get romping."

"Down!" gasped Carlos, flopping Peppy into the lying position. "Good boy!"

Okay, he was willing to lie still, anyway. But every time his young master put his arms around him, he started to tussle. "Say *'NO!'* like you mean it!" Greg instructed. "You're laughing, and Peppy thinks you want to play."

Carlos forced himself to get serious. And then the dog caught on. When he gave the command, Peppy dropped like Roxy had.

Whew!

Meanwhile, Mike caught onto this command the fastest. The Maltese was easy enough for its master to down, but it never stayed there. It kept rolling over and waving its front legs, as usual. Or hopping up and running. Kipsy's mistress hadn't gotten her to sit yet, so she could hardly get her to lie on her stomach.

And then there was Charlie! Stan had barely put his arm around his Great Dane's back when the dog whipped around and slapped his forelegs on the young man's shoulders. They both fell sideways, but only Charlie managed to keep his feet under him. He wound up straddling his master, pelting his face and neck and shirt with licks. Stan squinched his eyes shut and tried to push him away. "*N-o-o-o,* Charlie! Get *off,* Charlie!"

Greg rushed to the rescue, yelling *"NO!"* and giving his collar several sharp jerks. Stan rose to his knees, red-faced and messed up. "Any suggestions?" he gasped, wiping his face with the back of his arm and trying to look composed.

"Yeah. Before you come next time, take this big old boy (Greg clearly liked him) for about a two-hour run on the beach. In other words, *tire him out!"*

Stan accepted the napkin Becky rushed to give him and dabbed his face and neck with it. "That sounds like a plan," he sighed, reaching over and scratching Charlie's chest. The giant dog licked his hand lovingly.

Their assignment, besides practicing all the commands they'd learned, was to have their dogs sit-stay and down-stay for three minutes *without their leashes*—provided they were doing the commands perfectly while leashed. Peppy was ready—Carlos knew it!

"Did you bring that form you talked about?" he asked the trainer after the class was over.

"Oh, yeah! Sure." Greg whipped open the cardboard folder he carried and rifled through the rumpled stack of papers inside. "Yeah! Here it is." He shook his head. "I gotta get better organized."

He handed the green, four-page form to the boy. "The American Kennel Club is the organization that controls the registering of purebred dogs in this country."

Carlos looked confused, so Greg explained further. "Registering is where the club—called the AKC for short—lists a dog's name in its files, plus any awards it's won, plus the dog's parents and grandparents and so on, and *their* awards. These records prove that the dog is a *pure* golden retriever, or whatever, and that it doesn't have any collie mixed in, for example. Okay, so far?"

Carlos nodded, and Greg went on. "It's sort of like the U.S. government having your birth records to prove you were born an American. And just like the government gives you a social security number that identifies you, the AKC gives dogs registration numbers. Follow?"

Most of this was going into Carlos' brain. He'd have to think about it for awhile to really get it.

"See, the problem with Peppy is, nobody knows who his parents are. And nobody ever will. But the AKC won't register a dog as purebred unless it knows things about its mother and father—if they were purebred goldens themselves, and healthy and trainable. In order to keep the golden retriever breed pure and strong. Still getting it?"

"Yeah," said Carlos uncertainly.

"So the AKC will never register Peppy as a purebred golden retriever that could have golden retriever *puppies.* They don't know how pure his breeding is, and they aren't going to risk him giving a sickness to his puppies that he got from his father, for example."

Carlos shrugged. "He can't have puppies. The vet told me whoever owned him before me did that operation that makes it so he can't."

"He's been neutered. I'm glad to hear that. See, the AKC won't let any dog enter their obedience competitions without a number that identifies the dog. That's what an ILP number is for. It stands for Indefinite Listing Privilege. It means the American Kennel Club will list Peppy in their files and assign him his own number, even though he can't be registered as a purebred golden retriever. But to get an ILP number, he has to be neutered."

"So he can compete?"

"He sure can."

Good! That was all Carlos needed to know. He scanned the form. It didn't look too hard; he'd have to write down the reason why Peppy couldn't be registered as purebred. He'd explain, "Because I found him in an alley and I don't know who his mom and dad are."

He'd need to have two pictures taken of Peppy for the AKC files. Papa had a little snapshot camera that he used for family pictures. Maybe he'd let the boy borrow it.

It wasn't until he read the last line of the form's instructions that dismay hit him. "It says I gotta pay a twenty-five dollar fee to get Peppy his ILP number!"

"There are a lot of other expenses that go with training a dog for an obedience trial, too," said Greg. He placed a sympathetic hand on the boy's shoulder. He'd obviously guessed Carlos' problem.

"I can't enter Peppy in any competitions then! My family can't afford it, and I sure don't have the money! Stan's already paid for this class, and Miss Lindstrom bought Peppy the collar. I'm not gonna ask them to pay out *more*."

His newfound dream crashed around him like a house in an earthquake. He handed the form to Greg and walked away quickly so the man wouldn't see his eyes getting wet. Peppy heeled, keeping pace with him just the way he was supposed to.

As if it mattered anymore.

Mashell stood on the playground, alert for any acts of kindness or meanness in the kids milling around her. Her eyes rested on someone who was doing neither. Someone who looked like she needed some kindness *given* to her.

Judy Choi was sitting by herself on a bench, looking ready to cry.

"Hi, girlfriend," said Mashell, plopping beside her. She already knew what was bothering her. "Your family's store doin' any better?"

Judy shook her head. "I think the whole neighborhood is against us now. Hardly anybody comes to shop anymore. Dad says we've lost a lot of money." Her voice shook with anger. "And as if that's not bad enough, somebody smashed our back-door window with a rock last night."

The girl's eyes were filling with tears that she fiercely blinked away. "I've been praying that Jesus would stop all these people from hating us. But it's not working. Maybe He doesn't care . . . ." Her voice trailed away, and Mashell knew by the look in her eyes that she didn't need to correct her friend. Judy was about to do it herself. "I guess it's not His fault that people are so hateful," she murmured. "If they were good and loving, He wouldn't have had to die on the cross."

She sighed. "Maybe it's just as well the store goes out of business. Then we can move away from here."

"Wish I could help," murmured Mashell, squirming. The thing was, she knew exactly why nobody was shopping at Century Market. Mom had told her the Gordon Brown residents' committee, at the strong leading of Mrs. Ethel Johnson, had put out a notice urging people to boycott the store. As long as the Chois owned it, anyway.

Mashell could almost hear Mrs. Johnson ranting now. "They don't care about us, no *sir!* They just wanna bleed us dry for their own selfish benefit. Well, I say let's get somebody in the store that's one of us—that'll have a *heart* for us. You know what I'm sayin'?"

Mashell wasn't about to tell Judy all this—she was in enough pain. So she grappled to find something positive to talk about. "These—uh—messages we Hate Fighters givin' out been doin' wonders here at school . . . ."

Judy stood and grabbed her soft pink backpack. "But then there's the rest of the world. I gotta go, okay? My teacher wanted me to come to class early 'cause I gotta make up a test I missed." She started to walk away, then stopped and turned. "I don't want to move away from you and the rest of the Good News Club, though. You guys are my friends."

She left. *Father God, please help the Chois,* Mashell prayed. Judy was right. God wouldn't control the way people behaved. They were making their own choices for good or evil. Evil, in this case.

She stood with a heavy sigh and saw *another* person looking depressed. "Hey, Carlos," she called. He was leaning against the wall in the roofed-over bicycle court. She strolled toward him and plopped her backpack beside his stack of school books. (Her pack was light blue with a faded picture of Aladdin and Princess Jazmine on it. Way old, and way too young for a sixth grader. But what could she do? She had to carry her stuff in something!)

"What's up?"

His voice was as sober as his face. "Nothing."

"Given away any Hate Fighter slips lately?"

"I don't feel like it."

She decided not to ask why. Something was really bothering him, and she knew plying him with questions wouldn't help. She'd have to get him to tell her in a more roundabout way. *Just get him talkin' about anything, girl! Let's see . . . what he interested in?*

"How's Peppy comin' with his trainin'?"

Carlos turned his back to her, shaking his head, and one quiet, bitter laugh escaped him.

Bingo! "Not so good, huh?"

He turned around again, and the pain in his eyes made her feel sad, too. "He's doing great! That's what makes it hurt so much."

He paused, and she patiently waited. He'd tell her. All she had to do now was listen.

"Getting him an identification number and all that, it's going to cost a *fortune,* man! I can't enter him in obedience trial competitions 'cause there's no way my family can afford it. And *I* sure don't got the money!"

She winced in sympathy. She could relate completely.

"I'm still practicing with him 'cause he loves to do it, and I gotta get him ready for the class graduation. He's gonna be a star at something, anyway! But it's just *killing* me, you know? He's the *best!* And I'm the only one who'll ever know it!"

Mashell glared at him. "What do you call *us? Cat* litter?"

He smiled finally. "I mean besides my friends and family. In the *dog* world, you know? I mean, he deserves to have all kinds of awards printed after his name in that big list they got at the American Kennel Club. Only he ain't lucky, 'cause he's owned by a *ghetto kid."*

Mashell had been acting disgusted. Now she started to *feel* that way. *"Who's* given him more love than anybody could have on this whole earth? *Ain't lucky!* That dog's got the best master in the world! You think he'd be happy with anybody else? An' who rescued him, anyway? What if he hadn't been *found* by you? What you *mean* he ain't lucky!"

The girl was talking faster and louder by the second. Carlos held up his hands and backed away, looking scared.

But she could tell he was teasing. "Okay, okay. I get the message. You don't need to bite my head off, man."

She rolled her eyes and chuckled. "You know who I sounded like just now? My *grandma!*" They both laughed. "Aw man, there's gotta be somethin' we can do, you know what I'm sayin'? Maybe get you a job or somethin'."

"I've been thinking a lot about that. But all my ideas just kind of get blown away. Like, Mama and Papa won't let me sell papers 'cause they say it's too dangerous around here. They won't let me sell lemonade or nothing 'cause they're afraid somebody'll rip me off. And I wouldn't make enough, anyway. It would take *forever* to get twenty-five dollars. And that's just to get Peppy an ILP number."

"Number?"

"I'll explain later."

He obviously didn't feel like telling her, so she gave up and poured herself into thinking. "How 'bout *doin' stuff* for people, like mowin' old ladies' lawns?"

"Papa does all that in our neighborhood, besides going to the suburbs. He needs the money to feed us."

"How 'bout cleanin' people's houses? Washin' their windows? Sweepin' floors and cleanin' bathrooms and vacuumin'—"

"Anna and Mama do all that!"

Mashell gave him a dirty look. "Don't you go callin' it *girl stuff!* It's hard work!"

"I never said it wasn't! I just don't know how to do it!"

"You ever clean your dad's truck? Well then, you can about clean anything!"

He didn't seem to be listening anymore. He began to look excited. "Washing *cars!* That's what I could do! I could carry our hose around and hook it up wherever, and bring along soap and towels and stuff. This smog, it makes everybody's cars look dirty! I bet I'll find lots of people who wants their cars looking good again!"

It was a great idea. "I'll help. I like doin' stuff like that, especially if it's a hot day an' I got a swimsuit under my shorts. I bet Felipe and Bronce an' the other Hate Fighters gonna feel the same way. An' I *guarantee* Anna'll do it. When she don't gotta baby-sit."

He stared at her. "But don't you want some of the money?"

"Not *me*. I wanna see that dog of yours win an award!

Besides, goin' 'round askin' people if we can wash their cars'll give us Hate Fighters a chance to give out more yellow an' blue slips. We'll be gettin' *out* there, you know? An' we'll be safe 'cause there'll be a lot of us!"

Carlos looked more amazed the more she talked. And more cheerful. "Thanks, Mashell," he finally murmured. "Thanks a lot."

She grinned. *Mission accomplished!* School was about to start. She grabbed her pack and Carlos scooped up his books—and bumped her between the shoulders.

"Oh, sorry," he mumbled.

She didn't bother responding. He hurried toward his fifth-grade-class wall, and she ambled across the playground to join the sixth graders. A shout stopped her halfway across. It was Felipe, panting and red faced. He'd been playing a hard game of wall ball. He ran to her and yanked something off her sweatshirt. "You got something stuck on your *back,* you know?"

He handed it to her with a grin, and she suddenly felt warm all over. It was a yellow square of paper with John fifteen, seventeen written on it. In her own handwriting, even.

* * * * * * * *

The rock throwers were at it again. This time they were hiding behind a large bush with tiny leaves and even tinier white flowers on it, growing against the outside of Fern Street Elementary's wire-meshed fence. School had just gotten out, and they were flinging something at the passing kids. Something that bounced off their heads and backs and made them yelp, but not scream or bleed or anything that drastic.

Carlos and Felipe gave each other sly glances. "Let's check out what they're throwing," whispered Carlos. He dropped down and scuttled on all fours along the low evergreens growing on the inside of the playground fence. Felipe was right behind him.

They reached the three fifth graders who were laughing with muffled glee and giving each other hand slaps with each hit they scored.

They kept pulling rust-colored *somethings* out of the small outer pocket of a backpack that had—of all things—Batman on it. One of the things fell to the ground. As large as a walnut, shaped sort of like a fat teardrop and covered with hard wrinkles. A peach pit!

What have they been doing? Saving up pits since Christmas? thought Carlos in disgust. He didn't want to *know* what the inside of that backpack was like. He reached in his pocket and Felipe nodded in excited agreement. *Let's give these guys a message!*

Sticking the blue warning on the backpack *without getting caught* was going to be tricky. *You can do it. You did it before,* Carlos coached himself.

The mesh was too tight for him to jam his arm through. But the backpack was leaning against it, and all he'd have to do was work the fabric through a gap in the wire until he had a large enough chunk on his side. Large enough for a sticky note, that is. Then he'd push it back through carefully so the paper wouldn't get torn off by the fence.

Ooh! This was going to take some skill! He pursed his lips, waited until all three of them were throwing, then reached his thumb and two fingers through the fence. He pinched the pack and pulled ever so gently—

Whoa! The pit throwers whirled toward the fence and jammed their hands in the pack's outer pocket, intent on filling their fists with more ammunition. Carlos pulled away just in time! He and Felipe knelt behind the closest evergreen, frozen and hardly breathing.

And the pit throwers went back to their "game." Carlos rolled his eyes and crept toward the pack. *Hurry up, man! Before they run out of pits again! Easy now . . . don't draw their attention!*

Felipe was waiting with the blue paper poised in his fingers, ready to slap it on as soon as a large enough bit of the pack came through the fence. They were a team.

Okay! Carlos now gripped a fist-sized piece of black canvas. Felipe jammed the message on it and they both worked feverishly, trying to ease it back through without losing the note . . . .

And they were concentrating so hard they forgot to watch the pit throwers. A hoarse shout right above their faces made them both drop the pack and spring backwards like electric-shocked cats.

"What are you doing with my pack?" bellowed the threesome's leader. His name was Jose (pronounced Hoh-ZAY).

His friend caught sight of the blue square, still attached, and yelled, "Leaving wimpy 'I'm-better-than-you' messages!"

"The mysterious Hate Fighters!" sneered the third kid. "Too bad! Your secret is out! Everybody's gonna know who you are now!"

Jose formed his hands into fists and started walking toward the gate. "That's the least of their worries."

He broke into a fast run, with his friends alongside him. Carlos and Felipe gave each other one quick, scared look that said all they needed to say.

We're outta here, man!

Carlos bolted toward the nearest building, with Felipe pounding alongside him. The playground still held a small scattering of kids. *Grownup! Find a grownup!* Carlos ordered himself.

He angled toward a door at the end of the kindergarten wing. "Maintenance" said the plaque stuck in the upper-middle of it. The door was closed tight, and it was probably locked. As if he and Felipe wanted to wind up trapped in a janitor's closet!

Mrs. Murray's second-grade room was next to it, and her door was open. Carlos shouted her name and jammed his head in the door—only to see a deserted classroom. *Oh, boy!* The pit throwers were nearly on top of them! He and Felipe took off again.

The other doors along this wing were closed, and there was no time to check each one to see if anyone was inside.

Their only option was to *keep going.* Thank goodness they were both *fast.*

Why was there never a teacher around when you needed one?

"Our class!" gasped Felipe. "Maybe Mrs. Kane—" He didn't finish his sentence because he needed his breath for more important things, like running for his life. Carlos knew what he was going to say, anyway, and agreed with him. *Oh, man!* The pit throwers looked like they wanted to kill them. The two boys shot across the playground to the upper elementary wing.

Only to find their own classroom locked and empty. Carlos' mind was racing as fast as his feet. *Where's a guaranteed grownup place around here . . . ? The office! Of course!* Even if all the teachers were in a meeting or something, there was always somebody at the front desk to answer the phone and whatnot.

Big problem, though. To reach the office they'd have to turn around and head *toward* the pit throwers. They'd just have to lead them in a big circle. "Office," he panted to Felipe, who nodded and changed direction with him.

Suddenly Carlos felt a sharp sting on the side of his head. A peach pit clattered on the cement. Another clacked against a nearby wall. Then another hit his left shoulder. Felipe was getting struck too. Oh brother! Was this the pit throwers' answer to *everything?*

Ow! Those things hurt! At that moment, two things happened—the last door in the upper grades wing swung open (behind Carlos and Felipe) and Principal Dixon, holding a coffee mug and looking back over his shoulder, stepped outside. He was talking to someone. "Yeah, I'm heading to the meeting right now. If he calls before five, tell him I'll call him back today-*AYY!!!"*

His words turned into a bellow of shock and pain that stopped all the kids in their tracks. A pit had struck the lip of his mug, tipping it and splattering hot coffee all over the man's hand and the sleeves of his shirt and suit coat, not to mention his pants. He searched frantically for a place to set the mug, plopped it on a brick windowsill and turned to scan the playground with a baleful glare.

He shook the near-boiling liquid off his hand and kept shaking it to cool it. He used his other hand to snatch a handkerchief from his suit pocket. He hurriedly wiped his hand and sleeves and pants, and his voice thundered, not unlike Charlie's. *"Who's throwing things on the school grounds!"*

Carlos didn't expect the pit boys to answer. In fact, they'd turned and were racing away as fast as they could. Which was a dumb mistake, because it showed Principal Dixon exactly who'd done the wrong. His voice continued loudly, but in a calm, businesslike tone that had a knife edge to it—that made any kid who heard it tremble. "Mr. *Alvarez,* Mr. *Guerrero* and Mr. *Torres,* I'll see you in my office. You can stop running and come now or keep running and see me tomorrow. If you choose the second option, you'll lose an extra week of playground time."

The pit throwers stopped and came to him. *Good choice,* thought Carlos. He was feeling deeply relieved, and now it was his turn to be gleeful. Mr. Dixon noticed him and Felipe. "I take it you boys are watching this for a reason?"

"We're their targets," answered Felipe.

"Uh-huh. You want to come along too, and tell me about it?"

Mr. Dixon wasn't asking. The five boys wound up marching in stiff silence in front of the man, who was still trying to dab coffee off his clothes. Even his tie had splotches on it. The teacher he'd been talking to stuck her head out the door. "Should we start the meeting without you?"

"Yeah. Plan the hall-decorating contest. I've never been any good at cutting and pasting anyway. And Mrs. Harris, grab my coffee mug off the windowsill, if you please."

"I take it you'd like a fresh cup."

"You got *that* right!"

* * * * * * * *

Mr. Dixon sat with his deep brown fingers interlocked on top of his desk. He'd wasted no time doling out correction to the three throwers. They had to clean up every peach pit and, while they were at it, every scrap of litter off the playground, including under the bushes and behind them. They were to miss recess for the rest of the week too. "You could have knocked somebody's eye out, or worse," he scolded.

Now he was focused on Carlos and Felipe's part of the fracas. The blue message square that had started the chase sat on his desk in front of his hands. He regarded it with interest, and Carlos wondered if he wasn't amused, too. "So you guys are the mysterious Hate Fighters."

"There are more of us," said Felipe.

"I figured that. We've had dozens of these things show up."

Mr. Dixon picked up the paper. "Let's see. This is a blue one, and it's a scolder. To let kids who *aren't* being nice know it. And then, the ones that you give to nice people are . . . ."

"Yellow," answered Carlos.

Mr. Dixon studied the message again. "It's not a bad idea, really. Kids sure love getting the yellow papers." He looked at the pit throwers. "But it's a bummer getting a blue one, isn't it."

Not one of the three boys answered him. He went on. "Because it shows you the truth about yourself, and you don't want to face it. 'Okay, so I'm being mean,' you tell yourself. 'What of it?' "

Mr. Dixon leaned back. "This slip tells you Somebody really important thinks it's a big deal."

Jose Alvarez glared at him without being too cheeky about it. "I thought this was a public school, and you can't talk about God here."

"As a school principal, I have to respect all people's beliefs. These slips don't violate that, in my opinion. However . . . ."

He looked sternly at Carlos and Felipe. "People don't like to be criticized. They may even get mad enough to hurt the people criticizing them. You found that out the hard way this afternoon."

No lie, thought Carlos. His head still stung a little. Getting hit by a pit was better than getting beat up, though.

"So from now on stick to sneaking out compliments here at Fern Street Elementary, and let us grownups handle the mean kids."

Carlos' eyes went wide. "Sneaking? You mean you'll keep us a secret?"

A smile touched the corners of his lips. "I will. But I'm not the only person in this room."

Carlos glanced at the pit boys. It was obvious they planned to tell everybody they could who the Hate Fighters were. At least two of them anyway. Oh well. Maybe more kids would join . . . .

Mashell sat in the Hernandez kitchen, helping Anna feed Rosa by catching the bits of roasted chicken, boiled carrots and toast the toddler was dropping from her highchair tray. She used a washcloth, of course. No way was she going to touch soggy, half-chewed food barehanded.

She could hardly believe it. Over half the school wanted to join the Hate Fighters! Carlos and Felipe said that kids started pestering them the very next day—after they got over gloating that they knew who the Hate Fighters were.

"We can't write out that many notes, girlfriend!" she wailed to Anna. "How many hands they think you an' me an' Judy an' Bronce *got?"*

Anna remained calm. "They can write out their own, then. I think this is *great.* The notes are catching on at junior high, too. I think I'll get a couple of my school friends . . . *whoa,* Rosa!"

The toddler nearly dumped a sipper-cup of milk down her front. Anna caught it and steadied it while the baby girl grasped the handles on each side—with sticky, crumb-coated hands. She took a huge drink, then pushed the glass away with a happy sigh and smiled at her big sister. Her large, dark eyes narrowed to slits as the grin pushed her fat cheeks into them. Anna kissed her black curls and Rosa giggled.

"*I* sure wouldn't kiss her face right now," muttered Mashell. "Gross!" Her panic faded. Anna was right—this was *great!* Maybe they really were training folks in their world to love, not hate. "Mr. Dixon won't let us pass out no more blue warning notes at school, though. Just the compliments."

"I never did give out any of the blue ones. I'm not very good at telling people they're doing wrong."

Mashell put her arm across her friend's shoulders. "Girl, you just too much of a softy." Rosa, crooning, leaned over and rested her head on Anna's arm. She agreed completely.

This warm and wonderful scene was blown apart in the next second as Carlos burst in the door, all excited. "Anna, you should see Peppy! He's heeling all over the place, and he's not on the leash! I haven't had him on the leash for *any* of this practice!"

"Hey, Hernandez, when we gonna start washin' cars?" demanded Mashell.

"When Peppy and I are done practicing. We don't got much left to do."

Anna was busy wiping Rosa's face and neck and arms and hands. "I'll help you. Mama said she'd be back in ten minutes and then I can go."

Carlos looked pleased. "Felipe said he'd join us, too."

"You got until your mom gets back," said Mashell, rapidly cleaning up the mess from the tray and chair and floor.

He glared at her in mock disgust. "Since when did you become the boss?"

"Since I decided you need a business manager."

* * * * * * * *

They only found one car they could wash in the whole neighborhood, and the man talked them down to three dollars for it. (They'd started out asking five.) "You'll never get any business if you charge that much," he warned them. "I can get it done at the Spiffy Car on Avalon for two-fifty."

"But we do a deluxe job," Mashell tried to insist. The customer didn't budge.

"Some business manager," muttered Carlos to Felipe. Pretty discouraging. The heavy hose was making his shoulder ache, too.

"Maybe we could set ourselves up in an empty parking lot along Century and yell cars to us. I've seen other kids do that, you know?"

Mashell brightened up. "Yeah! Like church teens raisin' money to go to Colorado or somethin'."

"We could put up a couple big signs," suggested Anna.

Carlos squelched the idea, not because he wanted to argue, but because they needed to get practical. "But where? And don't you gotta have a permit or something?"

Nobody answered for a moment. "Maybe we can find a store owner that'll let us wash cars on his parking lot," said Felipe.

They all came up with the same name at once. "The Chois!"

The four kids hurried to Century Market. It had no customers. Mashell bought a pack of gum, just to give them *some* business.

Mr. Choi said they could wash cars on the empty lot next to the store. He let Carlos attach his hose to the outside spigot and even donated some big sheets of cardboard and magic markers for the three girls (Judy wanted to help) to turn into advertising.

Soon the five kids had spread themselves along both sides of the block, holding posters, waving wash rags, and yelling *"C-a-a-a-r wash!"*

They got two customers pretty quickly, and they worked fast and hard—and got wet shoes and shirts. But they did good work. Carlos sprayed the water (he'd promised Papa he'd take good care of the hose), and the others wiped the cars with soapy rags. Then he rinsed and they all dried.

"The secret is payin' attention so you don't miss no spots. An' polish all the metal so it shines," Mashell coached them. "An' don't use your dryin' towel once it gets dirty or soakin' wet."

It was a good thing Mrs. Choi had a bunch of extra rags at the store.

The second driver, a lady, gave them a dollar more than the three they asked for. Carlos added the cash to the growing wad in his pocket. "This is great, you guys!" he exulted. "I'll have twenty-five dollars in no time!"

Mashell raised her eyebrow at him. "But you can't stop there! Didn't you say there was a bunch of other expenses you gotta cover if you want Peppy to compete?"

"Yeah," Carlos admitted.

"Then keep yellin' up business!"

He nudged Felipe. "Man, what a slave driver!"

"Business manager!"

They'd just waved a third car, a red Buick, to the hose when an African-American man wearing dark sunglasses and all dressed in black ran past the parking lot toward the store. Carlos caught a glimpse of him flinging his arm out and saw something hurtle through the air. The left picture window of Century Market shattered inward. The man raced toward the fence behind the store, hoisted himself over it and was gone.

The boy dropped the hose, stunned, as shrieks carried from the store.

"Mom! Dad!" cried Judy, running for the door.

Mr. Choi blocked her and pushed her back outside. "*Stay out!* It's started a fire!"

"*What has?*"

Mrs. Choi was outside now. She gripped her daughter's shoulders, turned her around and made her run ahead of her. "Get! Get! We gotta get away from here! *Now!*"

She was not one to argue with at the moment. She waved fiercely at the four other kids and the Buick driver, beckoning them to run across the street with her. They all obeyed but the driver. "Somebody threw an incendiary device?" he yelled. "A pop bottle with a burning rag stuffed in its top and gasoline inside—"

"Yeah, yeah!" she answered sharply.

"I'll call 9-1-1!" He jumped in his car and roared away.

Judy found a voice to scream with. *"D-A-A-A-D!"*

"It's okay. He'll be okay. He's using the fire extinguisher!" Mrs. Choi was trying to keep her daughter calm, but Mashell saw her begin to shake. Smoke trickled through the broken window and out the door. The lady peered at the store, keeping her body between it and her daughter even though they were well across the street. She suddenly broke into frantic, loud Korean. Mashell didn't need to understand the language to know she was ordering her husband outside *now!*

She longed to see what was going on, but Mrs. Choi wasn't about to let her or any of the kids in close enough. All she could do was wait anxious minutes that felt an hour each. Judy started to shriek in Korean, too.

The smoke grew thicker and grayer. Its acrid, stinging smell carried across the street. At last Mr. Choi stumbled, gasping, from the store.

His wife scurried forward and hustled him across the street. Judy threw her arms around him. He still held the extinguisher in one hand. He put his other arm around her stiffly, looking hollow and drained.

He was a man in shock. He stared at the store and poured out a stream of Korean. Then he turned to the four kids and raised his shoulders as if he needed to apologize. "I couldn't stop it," he babbled. "I tried to fight it, but it spread so fast. So *fast!*"

He was cut off by a rumbling crash. Something had collapsed inside the store. Sparks shot out the open door and the gap in the window. They were followed by fast-flickering orange and blue flames growing taller with each passing second.

Carlos watched the firefighters scramble into position and signal the man on the truck to start the water pump. He'd seen them before, in their black rubber boots and pants and coats with a broad yellow stripe across their backs, wearing hard helmets with wide brims draping over their backs.

A small crowd had gathered to watch in curiosity and mute sympathy. A police car pulled up to fend away looters and protect the firemen. Judy was crying in her mom's arms now, and neither Mr. or Mrs. Choi said a word.

Carlos prayed nobody would get hurt and that they'd put the fire out before it spread to other buildings—before it completely destroyed Century Market. The firefighters had arrived quickly. But the fire, like a massive dragon, devoured the store and all within it more quickly still. It was shocking to see flames coming out the roof. And to watch the outer walls grow black.

Yet the fire dragon was doomed even as it roared its defiance. The fighters wielded their hoses like tubular swords and stabbed at its heart. And the flames, wherever they showed themselves—licking at the base of the walls or shooting through gaps in the roof—were beaten back and done away with by high-pressure spears of water.

And then it was over. The gray, billowing, stinging smoke was now replaced by hissing, nasty-smelling steam. Slimy, black puddles stood on the sidewalk and in the empty lot. Water dripped from the door and window frames. Century Market still stood, but it was now a sorry looking, black-streaked shell with only part of a roof.

The policeman ordered everybody to leave, including the kids. "But we're friends of the Chois," said Mashell meekly.

It was clear he didn't care if she was the president's daughter. *"Get moving!"*

Even Mashell knew better than to argue with an officer using that tone of voice.

The Chois were gathered around the officer's partner, probably making a statement about the guy who started the fire. *Lord Jesus, will you let them catch him?* Carlos prayed.

The four kids strolled away in silence. Suddenly Felipe blurted out, "They really got the fire out quick, man!"

"But even so, look how much damage it did," said Anna. "I hope the Chois aren't ruined now. I hope they can fix up the store again and keep it open."

"An' *I* hope people will stop bein' pig-headed an' start shoppin' there!" Mashell added hotly. "What's that guy's *problem* anyway, settin' it on fire! What *good* did it do him?" She proceeded to rant and rave against all the racism and hatred in Los Angeles. As if the city could hear her. Or would listen to her.

It wasn't that Carlos disagreed with Mashell, or felt less angry over the terrible thing the arsonist did to the Chois. But watching the firefighters work had impressed him, and Felipe's comment got him thinking along those lines. When she paused for a breath, he grabbed his chance to get a word in edgewise. "Could I ever clean a car fast with one of those hoses!"

Felipe gave an impressed nod. "You'd take off the first layer of paint, man!"

Suddenly a horrible thought hit the young businessman. *"Hose!* Oh, *man!* I left Papa's hose hooked to the side of the *store!"*

The kids stopped walking and stared at each other in horror.

"We gotta go back!" insisted Mashell.

Carlos bit his lip. "But that officer! He'll give us the chew-out of our lives if he sees us! He may even *arrest* us, you know?"

"Maybe we can sneak around behind, through the alley," suggested Felipe.

It was worth a try. The kids doubled back, turned left at the next cross street and, making sure no one was watching, scooted to the head of the alley leading to the back of Century Market.

The afternoon was waning into early evening. The sunlight wrapped everything in orange-gold light and shadows were long. The alley itself was half cloaked in darkness.

Carlos didn't like the reason for the darkness *at all.* Two dilapidated, wooden fences made of tall, flat boards, rounded on top, lined the alley on both sides. They were painted gray and were absolutely crawling with graffiti. There was a narrow, dark gap that ran between the right fence and the next building. Scraggly weeds grew tall in it and stretched feelers under the fence and into the alley itself. There was no side cover, and not much room to escape. The gravel-lined alley was only wide enough for one car or truck to go one way.

He held back. "Once we go in there, we're *committed.* Trapped, you know?"

Mashell shrugged. "It's *your* hose."

"No, it's my *papa's.*" That settled it. He led the way slowly, listening hard for anybody coming from either end of this wooden minicanyon.

They neared Century Market, where a gap in the left fence revealed the Chois' empty parking lot. He couldn't see the store yet. Suddenly he heard two sharp *whams* and the squeak of a door opening. He froze and so did the others.

Minutes later he heard excited whispers and feet running—*their way!* What should they do? Run back out of the alley? But they were so close to the opening! Yet if they went forward they'd meet the runners head-on, whoever they were. He had a strong feeling he didn't want to know.

Carlos jumped sideways and flattened his back against the right fence and beckoned the others to do the same. He inched sideways until he could see the empty lot . . . .

The runners were three teens: two guys and a girl. She carried a cardboard box mounded with things like cigarette cartons and beer cans and bags of peanuts and potato chips. One guy carried a calculator and a folding card table; the other held a small television to his chest and ran with the short, jiggling steps of somebody carrying something awkward.

Looters!

There was no question they'd taken these things from Century Market's storeroom. The fire hadn't done much damage to the back of the building. The storeroom door, now wide open, had plywood nailed over its window, and half of it was charred black and brittle. The other half was missing. The whams Carlos heard must have been the looters breaking it so they could reach in and unlock the door from the inside.

They were heading right toward the alley, totally unaware that four kids cowered against the fence. But they seemed well aware that police were stationed nearby, and they dashed headlong, hunched down and constantly peering around, especially over their shoulders.

A shout from somewhere made them stop for a second. "The alley!" one of them hissed. Sure enough! A policeman had entered it from the street side. And then another officer loped into the parking lot from Century Boulevard. The teens were trapped!

They flung down the things they'd stolen, turned tail and raced away. The TV smashed to the ground and flipped twice, nearly hitting Carlos, who sprang out of its way—into the arms of the policeman who'd come down the alley.

"Helping the looters keep watch or just waiting your turn?" he demanded angrily, clamping his hands on Carlos' shoulders.

The boy was so scared he babbled fast and high. "I ain't no looter, sir! An' I never saw those teens before. I'm telling the truth. I'm not lying to you! Don't arrest us! *Por favor?"* (Please? Pronounced PORE fah-VORE.)

Mashell valiantly pushed herself from the fence and came toward them. "He tellin' the truth. We ain't here to steal nothin'. The Choi family, you know, that owns this store? They our *friends.*"

The officer scowled at her. "I told you to *go home!* It's dangerous around here! Watch some tube if you want to be entertained."

"But I gotta get my papa's *hose,*" pleaded Carlos.

The policeman didn't ask him to explain what in the *world* he meant. He didn't look in the mood to hear it. His partner, who'd chased the real looters until it became obvious they were *outta here*, walked across the lot, talking in the breathy tone of someone trying to get his air back. "Well—at least we caught—*somebody.*"

Carlos poured out his frantic explanations all over again. The other officer stood with his arms folded, unconvinced. "Your pockets look pretty full, there. Empty them for me."

The boy obeyed instantly. Out came a rolled-up wad of dollar bills and two stacks of sticky notes.

"Where'd you get the money?"

He quickly explained about the car wash the Chois let him and his friends set up. He was cut off when the officer who'd caught him nudged his partner. (He'd let go of Carlos and was holding a stack of notes.) "Look at this. I think we just found our mysterious message giver!" He pulled a yellow sheet free and read what was written on the back. ". . . signed, the Hate Fighters."

Mashell grinned. "You been seein' our notes around?"

"*Your* notes? Yeah, I'll say we have. All over the place." Anna and Felipe had crept from the fence by now and were standing beside Mashell. The officer took them all in with a glance. "Are all of you these Hate Fighters?"

The four kids nodded. "'Bout half our school is by now!" added Mashell.

The two men glanced at each other, and Carlos saw a hint of a smile pass between them. "Not a bad idea," muttered the one who'd caught him.

The second officer had the other kids empty their pockets, too. Nothing but combs and used tissues and the crumpled wrapper from Mashell's pack of gum. And stacks of yellow and blue notes, of course.

The first officer finally smiled openly—as he ordered them to go home *now.* "But Papa's hose," Anna reminded Carlos softly.

"Where did you have it attached when you were running the car wash?" asked the second officer.

"There was an outside spigot on this side, near the front of the store," Carlos explained eagerly.

"No setting foot inside the burnt building."

"We won't, we *promise.* It should be right where we left it when the fire started . . . ."

"Find it and *get away from here.*"

The four kids scrambled to obey. Felipe was the first to spot it, but his eager shout changed at once to a groan. Carlos ran to him and groaned, too.

"What's the matter?" asked Mashell sharply.

Carlos picked up the hose so she could see for herself. The sprayer end was fine. But the end that had been attached to the now-blackened wall spigot was a blob of fused rubber, melted by the fire's heat until it separated from its metal fitting, which was still screwed onto the spigot. The hose was completely ruined.

He looped it over his shoulder, ignoring the soot and gravel it brushed onto his shirt, and walked away muttering.

"There goes my car-washing business. Now I gotta buy a new hose for Papa. I'll *never* earn enough money to compete with Peppy!"

Several days later the kids gathered after school to watch workmen knock away what was left of Century Market's roof. The city had sent inspectors to see if the whole building had to be torn down. It didn't, which was the first good news the Chois had heard since the fire.

Police had to watch the store around the clock to keep looters from cleaning out the place—not that there was much left that wasn't roasted, melted or soaked. Once the roof was gone the kids wanted to pitch in and help, but Mr. and Mrs. Choi insisted on clearing the place of all jagged and sharp things before they let their daughter and her friends go in.

The next afternoon, wearing their grubbiest clothes ("Which is mostly my whole closet," Mashell had said), she and Anna and Judy and Carlos and Felipe walked in the doorless front entrance and stared.

Mashell couldn't believe the difference. Afternoon sunlight angled down onto a debris-strewn, concrete floor that still had patches of curled tile attached to it. The refrigerator and freezing units stood silent, blackened by the same soot that covered everything and floated through the air in thick particles—that looked golden in the sunbeams, but stung her nose.

Most of the shelves had collapsed. The items on them—like cans and bottles and whisk brooms and half-burnt magazines—had fallen into haphazard piles. "You can throw away the canned goods," Mrs. Choi told the kids. So they tossed black-crusted stuff into garbage bags. Some cans still had labels Mashell could read even though the fire had burned away the colors and left only shiny lettering behind—pork and beans, tomato soup, corn . . . .

A few plastic bottles were still intact with dish soap or whatever inside them. Some had holes and near holes bubbled in them, with their contents dribbled all over their outsides. Some had turned into melted masses that looked like giant plastic amoebas. Mashell was glad Mrs. Choi had given all of them cloth gardening gloves to wear.

A little before five o'clock, Mrs. Choi insisted they go home. "You got supper waiting, yeah?" she said. "Don't be late for your moms. Thanks for the good work for us. Tomorrow's another day."

The five kids lugged the trash bags to the street curb for garbage collection. As Mashell plopped the last one beside the others, she glanced along the street. Her eyes caught a splash of yellow coming toward them on the sidewalk. Mrs. Ethel Johnson. There were two women with her, and all three of them were talking loudly. The girl could have sworn she heard one of them say something about the Chois . . . .

She looked at the other four kids. They'd heard it too, and there was anger in their eyes to prove it. Almost as one, they dropped to their knees behind the shiny black mound of bags. They needed to hear the rest of what these ladies were saying.

"Well, if you ask me," Mrs. Johnson was saying, "this mess here is God's judgment on 'em. Mm-hmm. That's what I think."

"Yeah, but I *did* hear it was started by—" began one of the others.

Mrs. Johnson went on as though her friend wasn't even talking. "They didn't have no call chargin' the prices they did."

"Burnin' the store down ain't right, though!" piped up the third woman.

"'Course it ain't!" snorted Mrs. Johnson. "I never said it was! But it was bound to happen. They don't belong here. Maybe now they'll get the message."

"Yeah," said the second lady with a slow nod. "It would be for the best if somebody else owned the store . . . ."

Mrs. Johnson glared at her watch. "Ladies, would you *look* at the time! We gonna be late for the meetin'!"

They walked faster and passed the trash bags without noticing the five kids crouched behind them. Judy sat tight-jawed. Mashell gave her and the others a steely-eyed glance. "Meetin'?" she whispered. "Let's follow 'em. I got somethin' to say to these people!"

Carlos pulled a stack of blue notes from his pocket. "We all do!"

* * * * * * * *

They wound up at Gordon Brown housing community's meeting room. The kids hovered half a block away, watching a crowd of adults walk into the very place where love and God's praise had flowed a few days ago during Good News Club. Mashell wondered what kind of feelings would fill the room now.

The door closed. A piece of paper taped to it said, "Residents' Committee Meeting, 5:00 - 6:00."

"Mama wants us for supper at six," Anna reminded Carlos.

Mashell needed to get home as well. But Grandma wasn't really expecting her until five-thirty. That left a little less than half an hour. "What we gotta say shouldn't take too long."

She led the way. The five kids walked in with Ronald Tompkins, who lived three units down from her. He held the door for them, looking surprised that five kids wanted to attend a meeting of the Gordon Brown residents' committee.

They'd placed ten chairs around two long tables shoved together end to end. Mashell recognized "her" chair among them by the curved brown scratch on the back. Mrs. Ethel Johnson was sitting on it.

Adults balancing coffee cups and donuts were making their way to join Mrs. Johnson. They also stared in amazement at the five children who walked quietly to lean against the book shelf that usually held their Good News Club snacks. Mashell noticed a few cringes among them as they caught sight of Judy Choi. Mrs. Johnson gave them a sharp glance, and Mashell saw her lips tighten.

Mr. Tompkins—he was the chairman—called the meeting to order. "Our first business," he said, "is to take a vote, in light of what's just happened, on whether we should cease the boycott of—" he looked at Judy and cleared his throat—"Century Market."

"You've been *boycotting* us?" the girl blurted out. Her eyes went wide with pain and shock.

Mashell winced. *I shoulda told her. Girl, you blew it again.*

Mrs. Johnson flicked her thumb back at the lineup of kids. "Say, what *is* this, lettin' them in here! How we s'posed to carry on an objective meeting with—"

Judy cut her off in a voice so filled with hurt she could only whisper. "*Why* are you doing this? You're ruining my family's life!" She took a deep breath and her voice came out with more strength, though it trembled. "We never did anything to hurt you! My parents are just trying to make a living! We live here now. *Why won't you accept us?"*

She ducked her head and Mashell watched hot tears drip down her cheeks. But she fought them away and kept from sobbing out loud. An uneasy silence filled the room.

And Mashell knew just how to fill it. She pulled two stacks of Hate Fighter messages from her pocket, marched to the table and plopped them in front of the chairman. "You prob'ly been seein' these things floatin' around. Well, we confess. We been the ones sneakin' 'em all over, cause *we* the Hate Fighters."

She looked back at her friends in triumph, then turned her gaze to the chairman. "Now, you grownups on this committee, you got two choices. You can either love the Chois by shoppin' at their store again, or you can hate 'em by not shoppin' there, which means they'll go outta business an' maybe even lose everything they got. While we was helpin' them clean up this afternoon, I overheard Mr. Choi say somethin' to his wife 'bout goin' bankrupt, an' I'm pretty sure that's what it means."

"It does," said Judy quietly. She was still wiping silent tears. "Dad says we're close to bankruptcy now. We might even have to leave our apartment."

Mashell gave a curt nod. "So, there you have it. Love 'em or hate 'em. If you love 'em, you all gonna get yellow slips from us, that say you did what Jesus said." She raised her hand to cue the other kids, and they recited, "John fifteen, seventeen. 'This is my command: Love each other.' John fifteen, seventeen."

"It's on the slip there," she added. "You can read if for yourself. An' the backside, too."

She had them pass a yellow slip around the table. Everybody read it but Mrs. Johnson, who handed it to her neighbor with a grunt of disgust. "If you *hate* 'em," the girl went on, "we gonna give you the blue slips sayin' you *didn't* obey God's command."

And that was that.

She walked back to the bookshelf and waited with her arms folded, like Mrs. Joyce waiting for the Good News

Club to behave properly. The chairman stood and was about to speak.

But Mrs. Ethel Johnson hadn't had her say yet. "Now just wait a minute!" she growled, slapping her palm on the table. *"Ain't* it easy for a mouthy kid to come marchin' in here givin' out orders! A child her age ain't gonna have a grasp of *money* and what it's like livin' on a fixed income. She just don't understand the way things are!"

Her voice grew louder and she started to wave her fist for emphasis, which made the saggy skin on the back of her upper arm wave back and forth. "Just 'cause we want somebody we can *trust* to be runnin' our neighborhood store don't mean we *disobeyin'* God's command!" She turned from the waist up and glowered at Mashell. "How *dare* you accuse me of *hatred!"*

Judy couldn't keep her feelings in any longer. A sob rushed out of her and she burst out, "But Mrs. Johnson, that's how it *feels!"*

Silence again. Anna patted Judy's back. The chairman scratched his neck and said quietly, "Oh, Ethel, I think these kids understand exactly the way things are."

They finished the vote in just a few minutes. Nine were in complete favor of ending the boycott immediately *and* helping the Chois back on their feet by painting and building shelves and other things that they couldn't afford to hire workers for.

One refused to vote.

Several weeks had gone by. Carlos and Peppy stood (and sat) on the sidewalk in front of their house, waiting for Stan to pick them up. "Last class, dog! You're gonna do *great* at the graduation exercises! Greg says two hundred is a perfect score. You can do it!"

Peppy looked up and grinned, and his tail slapped the grimy concrete. The boy petted his head and neck and sighed. "I sure wish I could enter you in the obedience trial coming up this spring. But I won't have the money yet. You understand, don't you?"

The dog panted with his mouth in a doggy smile but remained in a perfect sit. "I hate to let you down, but Greg says there are lots of other competitions. We'll get into one *someday.* I promise."

Peppy seemed to believe him completely. If only Carlos could make *himself* believe it. Maybe he'd feel less disappointed.

Suddenly the dog perked up his ears and breathed out, "Ruh!" In the past he would have pranced around Carlos, yelping in excitement. But now he put all his eagerness into his eyes and quivering muscles and remained sitting as long as his young master's command was in effect.

The boy decided to release him. Though he couldn't see or hear it yet, Stan's truck was about to come into view. Peppy's much sharper ears were picking up the familiar engine noises and he was anxious to greet his friends.

"Okay!"

The dog instantly hopped to all fours and barked, high and joyfully. The royal blue truck rounded the corner off Century Boulevard and pulled up to the Hernandez' house.

Stan and Becky were late, so they couldn't run the three dogs to get them settled down. Meaning Charlie, of course. The young man had to wrap his arms around the Great Dane's chest and shoulders to keep him inside while Carlos hurriedly kenneled Peppy. Then Stan struggled to latch the back gate shut while Charlie slammed it with his front legs. *"No! Down!"* bellowed Stan.

Ka-*thunk!*

They were on the move at last, with Carlos sitting sideways in the back space of the king cab, on a single seat that folded out from the wall and sat low to the floor.

They passed Century Market. The boy waved at Mashell and Felipe and Anna and Bronce, who were busy helping repaint the front of the store. They waved back and shouted and ran to the parking-lot side of the store to point at something, though he couldn't make out what they were saying. Or doing.

He'd find out after the class was over. He planned to help paint, too.

"I think it's great, how this whole neighborhood has pitched in to help the Chois," said Miss Lindstrom.

Carlos agreed. "Yeah! We've been giving out yellow slips all over the place!"

"Doing *what?"*

He winced. The Hate Fighters were still a secret to his Good News Club teachers, if not to many others around here. "Uh, just something."

She didn't pursue it. "Are the Chois doing okay now?"

"Yeah. They're getting lots of business, 'cause they're the only store in walking distance of Gordon Brown and lots of other neighborhoods around here. Nobody's boycotting them anymore."

"That's great!" said Stan.

Carlos gave himself a secret smile, because *he* knew why! "Only one thing though," he said. "Judy says her parents are still worried because the guy who burned the store hasn't been caught. And they're afraid he'll try it again or do something else to wreck them."

Miss Lindstrom shook her head. "Why would anybody . . . maybe the guy will quit trying to hurt the Chois now that he sees the rest of this part of Watts backing them up."

"I hope so," said Carlos.

Stan started talking about the upcoming dog graduation—hoping Charlie would be in the mood to obey that night, wondering whom he should invite. "My whole family's coming, and half the Good News Club," said Carlos.

The young man whistled. "We'll see how my big, lovable, way-too-playful boy does."

"He'll do *fine,*" Becky assured him.

She didn't need to give such assurances to the boy behind her. There was no question how Peppy would do—as long as his young master got the commands right. Suddenly Carlos felt nervous.

* * * * * * * * *

Greg ran the class as though it was the graduation itself, except he couldn't take the time to have each owner and dog complete all the individual exercises in front of everyone as they would on Wednesday evening. "Today you'll only do the 'stand for examination' by yourselves, with me judging you," he told them.

All right! Carlos mouthed to Peppy. He always did the stand perfectly, as long as his young master remembered everything *he* was supposed to do.

They were meeting in the place where the exercises would be held: the outfield of a baseball diamond with several rows of bleachers for the audience. Carlos stared, all curious, at the plastic yellow ribbon strung through holes in the tops of metal stakes. The stakes formed a large rectangle that got its shape from the ribbon running along the top.

"That's the ring," Greg told the class. "That's where the exercises will take place." He gave his youngest pupil a knowing glance. "And it's set up just like a ring at an obedience trial."

"Someday," muttered Carlos, stroking the top of Peppy's head.

"Remember to practice your dogs in front of people," Greg reminded the class. "They need to get used to distractions or they'll break away and run toward the crowd." He glanced at Charlie. "Especially if your dog likes people."

Stan leaned toward Becky, and Carlos heard him murmur, "I have a bad feeling about this. He's started jumping up again. He'll probably knock some old lady over and I'll get sued for a million dollars."

She couldn't give a sympathetic reply because Greg was going on with instructions. He wasted no time forming them into lines and shouting out orders. (He was going to be the judge Wednesday night.) "Don't expect any favors from me just because I know you and your dogs," he warned the class. "I'll be as tough on you as the judges at an obedience trial."

Carlos' hands grew moist. The first exercises were the combined "heel on leash" and "figure eight." Greg called out "Forward!" and the lines of dogs and people moved ahead as one. The boy made a mental promise to Peppy as they walked crisply, waiting to hear what direction the trainer wanted them to turn. *Dog, for the next couple days we're gonna practice like never before!*

Somehow he knew that Peppy was as eager to get a perfect score as he was.

* * * * * * * * *

Carlos jumped down from the king cab. He still felt elated. One hundred ninety-six! Only four points from perfect! Surely he and Peppy could iron out the tiny mistakes they made that cost them *four little points.*

He was so anxious to join the painting crew that he was having Stan and Becky drop him off at Century Market. There was some nice shade along the parking lot fence; he could tie up Peppy and keep an eye on him while he worked.

Charlie was as hyper as ever. It was going to be tricky, getting Peppy out of the truck and keeping him and Mike *in.* Stan decided he'd put his leash on Charlie before he put the gate down, to make sure the megadog didn't get away. He pushed open the top-hinged back window just enough to reach his dog's neck . . . .

He shouldn't have tried something new. Getting his leash on meant only one thing to Charlie—he was getting *out!* As soon as it snapped onto his collar, he gave a great, excited *"Hroof!"* and leaped *over* the back gate! Never mind that the window hung in his face. He'd shoved against it enough to know that if it wasn't latched to the gate, it would simply push outward when he hit it. And hit it he did.

He caught Stan completely by surprise. The young man gave a bellow as his dog's leap yanked him off-balance. The window slammed against his head and he pitched forward to his knees. The leash jerked loose from his hands. Charlie hit the pavement—a free dog.

Who could run faster than any human. Becky barely managed to catch Mike and slam the gate closed on him, or there would have been *two* dogs charging down Century Boulevard . . . with its people-filled sidewalks and heavy traffic.

All the young painters screamed and started running after him. Carlos raced after them with Peppy, hoping he could lure Charlie to a halt again. *"NO!"* hollered Stan, clasping the side of his head. *"Charlie, COME!"*

The Great Dane slowed a little, as though his conscience stung him for ignoring his master's voice. Oh, but running in this new place was just too much fun! He sped up with a snort.

Carlos held his breath and prayed as the dog pelted across the first cross street. Thank goodness, the light was green for him which meant there was no traffic in his path! Oncoming walkers scattered away from Charlie as though he was a runaway truck. Then they turned and stared, until the pounding feet of young runners caused them to leap sideways *again.*

A neighborhood store owner must have called the police, because a squad car pulled into the Century Market lot. The officers got out and studied the situation without a word to anyone.

"C-H-A-A-R-L-I-E-E, COME!" Stan kept bawling as he joined the chase.

And just like that, the Great Dane decided to obey! He stopped with a "*Wuff,*" bobbed once on his quivering legs and began to lope toward his master, who'd doubled his speed to pass the kids so he would meet the dog first. "Good *boy!*" he croaked. "You're *wonderful!*"

To Carlos' total relief, one of the officers hurried to the intersection and held the waiting cars at bay so Charlie could gallop back across it safely. No more traffic worries! In a minute, he'd be back on his leash and heeling safely beside Stan.

Except that something caught his eye. Charlie got his *oh boy, oh boy, oh, boy* look on his face again and angled away from his master toward the fence-lined alley leading to Century Market. Carlos thought he was going to charge down the alley, but instead, he scampered to the weed-filled gap between the right fence and the building it ran alongside.

It was barely wide enough for him, but Charlie trotted in anyway, with a wagging tail and a happy, low-voiced snort. There was *something* back there he wanted to play with. He totally ignored every command Stan yelled at him.

The something turned out to be some*body.* As Carlos ran back through the alley to the parking lot, he heard a man's voice, hushed and frantic. *"No!* Get *away* from me! Go home! NO! *Get DOWN!"*

Then he heard a *thunk* and the shuffles of somebody trying to wrestle off a playful Great Dane. Charlie continued to grunt with pure joy. Then the boy heard somebody break into a run.

He reached the lot just in time to see a man wearing dark glasses and dressed all in black burst from the gap and tear into the open. Then the man saw the police car and the two officers. He stopped cold, and as he turned back toward the alley Carlos saw shocked terror on his face. But only for a moment. Charlie bounded up to him, leaped up with his front legs and planted them on the man's shoulders. He wasn't prepared to be slammed into by one hundred fifty pounds of barreling dog. He went over backwards with a yell.

There was a crash. A sharp tinkling. Charlie moved in to lick the man's face, but suddenly he leaped clear of him with a *"Hwoof!"* of disgust. He sniffed the dark puddle spreading out from under the man's back, then jumped away again with a sneeze and loped toward his master, who was getting hoarse from shouting by now.

The officers were on top of the guy in a moment, dragging him to his feet and slamming him against the back of Century Market to frisk him. Carlos grimaced as he saw that the man's back and right arm were bleeding. Something had slashed open his shirt and cut him. The boy quickly caught on to what had done it.

The man had been carrying a glass bottle in his back pocket. It was all shattered now, but its top was still intact enough to hold the piece of rag he'd stuffed into it. Carlos drew close enough to catch a whiff of the liquid that had driven Charlie away. Not that he needed to smell it to know what it was.

Gasoline.

Charlie was the hero of the day. Everybody fussed over him, but Stan most of all. "Who would've known!" he babbled to Miss Lindstrom. "Who would've known my big, old, over-playful, *puppy*-at-heart would ever save somebody's grocery store from getting burned *the second time?"*

The Great Dane had finally gotten rid of his excess energy. He sat beside Stan, looking delighted, while Stan, looking even more delighted, slap-rubbed his back and chest.

The Chois insisted that Stan take home a beef roast to feed Charlie, as their reward to him.

"Thanks anyway, but that wouldn't be good for him. He eats special-formula dog food."

"Then we'll buy him a *truckful!"* said Mr. Choi.

The fire-starting man (he seemed about Stan's age) was arrested. "Wonder who he is an' what gripe he had against the Chois," Mashell said quietly as the kids watched him slump, handcuffed, into the back seat of the police car.

Felipe started making guesses. "Maybe he was jealous that *they* owned a business and he didn't. Maybe he was put up to it by somebody that wanted to own the store *themselves.* Maybe he's just a racist . . . ."

"Maybe we'll never know," said Carlos. "Anyway, the good news is, he ain't gonna get another chance to ruin the Chois' business." He saw Anna start to pray and questioned her with his eyes.

"I want him to learn that Jesus loves him and will forgive him for what he did," she explained. "If he asks Him to."

"A*men,* sister!" said Mashell. "Hey! Carlos, in all this fuss . . . you notice anything 'bout the store?"

Carlos gave her a confused frown. They were standing in front of Century Market. It had a fresh coat of clean, white paint covering most of it. Above the door, somebody had already blocked out the letters of the store name. In a few days they'd be filled in with bright red shadowed by blue. And then maybe the sign painter would add some tomatoes and celery and a wedge of cheese or maybe a carton of milk and a chunk of steak—to show the neighborhood what this store sold.

"The lettering?" he asked. What was she *driving* at? She was going to drag out the mystery as long as she could, he knew. Mashell gave a sly chuckle and so did the others. Was he the only one who didn't know what was going on? He sounded more irritated than he actually felt. "Just *show* me!"

She beckoned him to follow her, and the others fell in around him as they paraded from the front of the store to the side facing the parking lot. She pointed to the wall and said, "Okay, you been *showed.*"

He looked where she gestured and his eyes widened with surprise and pleasure. *"Cool!"*

The ugly graffiti that used to glare out from the side wall was now lost under a blanket of clean white. The sign man had painted two gigantic yellow sticky notes on the wall, with the first one's bottom edge curling out slightly and the second one's curling back. To represent the front and back of a note that was slightly crumpled from being carried in a kid's pocket.

The "front" page had John fifteen, seventeen painted on it—words that were totally familiar to Carlos by now. The "back" said, "The Hate Fighters obeyed Jesus' command. Let's join them."

"How '*bout* us Hate Fighters!" he blurted out. The other Good News Club kids joined him in a yell of triumph.

* * * * * * * * *

Carlos' heart beat faster with every owner and dog that entered the ring. He was *last.* Why did Greg *do* this to him? He could actually see his hands shaking. His mouth was completely dry.

Peppy looked calm and happy, panting easily and lying to the left of his young master, who sat fidgeting and grumbling silently about the hard bleacher seat and Mama constantly reaching over to smooth his dress shirt or straighten his bangs and why did he have to wait so *long?*

He had his friends' and his teen sister's total sympathy. "You two will do *great!*" they kept assuring him.

He hoped he and Peppy would do better than the other dogs and their owners.

Kipsy was given zero points for the heel on leash because she still insisted on dragging her mistress around. Other dogs were docked because they didn't match their masters' paces—they either failed to run during the "fast" order or failed to drop back to a walk for the "slow."

For the figure eight, Greg had two adult assistants stand facing each other, thirty feet apart, like human posts. The dogs were supposed to heel while they and their masters circled the assistants in a figure-eight pattern. The dogs were to *completely* ignore the two people, who stood rigid like Queen Elizabeth's guards. But the little Maltese kept rising on its hind legs and pawing at them. Big deduction.

Charlie stopped, sat, and offered his paw to "shake hands." Stan had to jerk his leash hard to get him moving again. Zero points.

Charlie did okay for the rest of the leash exercises, but as soon as Stan removed the restraint, he broke away and ran to the audience to greet all the *nice people*—who looked ready to run until they saw that the giant dog only wanted a back scratch. (Stan had very wisely taken him on a two-hour romp before the graduation began.)

Mike had done the best so far, but he was given zero points out of thirty for sitting down during the stand for examination—a mistake nearly all the dogs made. Carlos could hardly bear to watch. Greg docked Mike several more points for shifting his weight from paw to paw while he sat. Peppy did that sometimes . . . .

Mike had yet to be scored on the group exercises. None of the dogs and their owners had done them yet; they had to wait until the individual competition was over. *One more dog-and-master team to go before—our turn.* Carlos wiped his hands on his pants, and they went right back to feeling clammy.

It was the Doberman pinscher and his master. He was a different dog now. He never tried to attack others anymore, even when he was unleashed. He obeyed the commands well. The only mistake he made was during the "recall," but it was a big one. The exercise consisted of the dog sitting and staying while his master walked thirty-five feet away and faced him. When Greg ordered, "Call your dog," the man commanded, "Come!" The Doberman instantly trotted toward him. But he was supposed to stop and sit a few feet in front of his master, facing him, waiting for Greg to order "Finish." Then the man would have commanded "Heel" and he would have scuttled quickly behind his master to sit at his left side. He didn't. He forgot to sit in front of his owner and went directly to the heel position. Big deduction.

He got lots of applause anyway, and some generous pats and praise from his master. This Doberman was a *good* dog!

Lord, please help Peppy not to make that mistake, Carlos prayed, pulling away from Mama as she smoothed his hair again. *Don't let me make mistakes either!*

Our turn! He stood up, wondering if everybody could see his legs shake. He felt certain he'd mess up royally because he was too nervous to *think.* He looked down at Peppy, who looked back with a doggy grin and soft *"Ruh."*

And he felt a little better. He and Peppy had worked hard. They were a champion team already. The boy took a deep breath, did a split-second mental review of the commands and said, "Heel."

They walked briskly together to the ring and entered it through a gap left between two posts. Greg stood stone faced, holding a clipboard and pencil, as though he'd never seen this eleven-year-old student and his golden before. Carlos stopped and Peppy sat.

"Are you ready?" Greg asked curtly.

Carlos nodded.

"Forward."

"Heel." Peppy kept perfect pace, head up, chest out, eyes dancing, no matter what direction Carlos turned and no matter how fast or slow he went. By the time Greg said, "Exercise finished," Carlos wasn't nearly as nervous. Just keyed up. Totally alert. Concentrating as hard as he ever had in his life.

Peppy might have made a mistake during the figure eight. He looked up, flashed a doggy smile, and *huffed* at one of the assistants, and his walk slowed for the shortest of moments. Carlos would have had to turn his head to see if Greg marked a deduction on the score sheet—but that would have caused a bigger deduction still. Oh, well. He wasn't going to let it bother him. He refused to get rattled. *Keep going the way you're going. We're doing fine,* he told himself.

The golden stood like a rock for the stand for examination. He did the "heel free" (unleashed) flawlessly.

Now it was down to the last phase of the recall. Carlos had been standing and staring at his dog (he looked so far away!) for what felt like ten minutes. "Call your dog," ordered Greg.

Carlos yelled, "Come!" Peppy sprang forward joyously and loped to his young master. Then he sat square in front of him, laughing with his eyes. Carlos wanted to laugh, too!

"Finish," said Greg.

"Heel!" The boy couldn't keep the giggle out of his voice. Peppy snapped around behind him and sat at heel again, beside his master's left leg.

"Exercise finished," said Greg, breaking into a grin. "Well done!"

The boy laughed out loud now, and completely messed up all the careful grooming Anna had given Peppy beforehand. The audience clapped and cheered and hooted. Especially his friends.

But he had to get serious again. Time for the last two events: the group exercises of "long sit" and "long down." Greg had the owners and unleashed dogs line up in the ring. (He was absolutely straight faced again.) "Sit your dogs," he ordered them. All the dogs sat on command but

Queenie, the poodle. Her mistress had to push her bottom down. Big penalty.

"Leave your dogs."

"Stay!" the owners commanded, then walked from their dogs to the other side of the ring. Carlos prayed Peppy would still be in place, no matter what the animals around him were doing. He turned around. He *was!*

They all were, at the moment. But Kipsy, bored with the whole thing, flopped into the down position. So did a Dalmatian. So did Queenie. Zero points for all three. *I bet the other two are lying down 'cause they saw Kipsy doing it, and they figured if she could, they could too!* fretted Carlos. *Peppy, stay sitting!*

He did.

Charlie began to whine softly, yearning to come to his master. He quivered and leaned forward, threatening to break. Stan shook his head and raised his eyes to the sky. But the minute was nearly up. The Great Dane stayed!

"Back to your dogs," ordered Greg.

Stan nearly ran to him. All the owners hurried to walk around their dogs and come from behind them into the standard heel position. Another Dalmatian, happy that her mistress was approaching, broke loose and met her. Zero points.

Peppy looked thrilled to have Carlos back at his side, but he knew better than to move. The boy and the dog had practiced this exercise too much for him to do otherwise.

"Exercise finished," said Greg.

Stan was so thrilled that Charlie didn't break, he was practically babbling.

Carlos scratched Peppy's ears and whispered, "You're the *best!"*

The long down lasted for *three* minutes. It went badly for the Maltese, who did his usual roll-on-his-back-and-wave-his-legs. His owner shook his head and smiled. It was obvious he loved the little thing. Even when he disobeyed he was *cute.*

And then the worst happened. Something one of the other dogs did suddenly irritated the Doberman. It lashed out sideways with a snarl and a snap. Concerned gasps rippled through the crowd. Greg jumped on it instantly, ordering the Doberman's owner to remove him from the ring. The dog left calmly at a perfect heel, but first it had to get in a few sharp, barking insults to the offender.

Carlos shook his head in sympathy. Greg had been careful to keep the Rottweiler and the other large dogs away from the Doberman, so who . . . .

Kipsy! *"Girl!"* yelled her mistress. "What'd you go an' try to *bite* that dog's nose for? *Shame* on you!"

Kipsy had to leave the ring, too. But the damage she'd done spread beyond herself and the Doberman. Mike, rattled by the Doberman's angry attack, stood up and looked at his mistress as if to ask, *What do I do now?* Zero points.

Charlie stood too. And Queenie. The Maltese sprang up and ran to its master. Finally, Peppy was one of only three dogs still lying down! He had his ears raised and he was looking at his young master with questions in his eyes. Carlos grimaced. Should he give Peppy another hand signal for stay? Just a little *reminder,* so he wouldn't get up like the other dogs? That would be cheating . . . a violation called "double handling." He'd get docked almost to zero for it. *If* he got caught.

Greg wasn't watching him at the moment. The boy *hated* losing, and this wasn't fair! It wasn't Peppy's fault that a bratty little dog started a fight with the Doberman and got all the dogs upset! Peppy's body squirmed and Carlos' heart tightened. He was shifting his back feet to get them more squarely underneath him. He was preparing to stand up.

The boy formed his left hand into a fist. Just one quick flash of his flat hand and Peppy would get it and stay put. Just one . . . .

But the boy knew Jesus was watching—and He was more important than Greg! Carlos closed his eyes and relaxed his fingers and kept his left hand by his side. And prayed that his dog would lie still.

He didn't want to open his eyes because he was afraid he'd see Peppy standing up. Maybe even walking toward him. That would be a big zero. When was this exercise going to *end?*

"Back to your dogs," Greg finally said.

Carlos opened his eyelids enough to see Peppy still lying down with his haunches high on each side of his back and his forelegs stretched in front of him. His young master nearly yelled out with joy—but that would have caused a *big* deduction! Silently he breathed, *Thank You, God!* He hurried around Peppy and came to his side. The other two owners did the same.

"Exercise finished."

Graduation finished! Carlos sighed in relief and tousled the fur on Peppy's back. "Way to go, dog! You stayed! You *are* the best!"

The crowd generously applauded all the dogs and their masters as Greg had them line up in front of the ring. (Kipsy's mistress, all upset, wasn't going to. But Carlos watched Greg soothe her and make her feel good about herself and her dog again. All in two minutes. He'd obviously run into this kind of thing before.)

He spoke in a voice that carried to every person present. "These people have done a great thing with their dogs these past ten weeks. They've created animals that are enjoyable to be around. That are now better citizens than they were before. They can go on to more training, or they can stop with what they've learned and *keep practicing.*"

His word emphasis brought a chuckle from the crowd. "As for tonight, whether they received zero points or two hundred, these partners deserve a *hand.*"

The crowd broke into hearty applause. The Good News Club kids cheered. Then Greg raised his hand. "I'd like to give special recognition to three dogs that earned over one hundred points this evening."

The Rottweiler and his owner earned one hundred ten. Becky and Mike got one hundred thirty-seven. The Doberman and his master earned the highest, one hundred fifty. Greg called them to stand in front. More clapping. Carlos felt his face turning red. *Hey! Peppy earned over one hundred didn't he?* Carlos could have sworn he did the best! What was going *on?*

Greg raised his hand again. "Only one dog and his owner earned a qualifying score that would allow them to work toward the American Kennel Club title of Companion Dog if they had earned this score at an obedience trial competition. That is, this team received over fifty percent of the possible score for each exercise. They didn't get *any zeros,* and in most exercises they received a perfect score."

Carlos' face *really* turned red now.

Greg went on. "Qualifying, by the way, is one hundred and seventy points." He grinned. These two earned *one hundred ninety-two.* That's only eight short of perfect. It's the highest score I've ever given at a beginning-level, training-class graduation."

He turned and beamed at the youngest graduate, whose head was swimming. "Carlos and Peppy, get up here."

Papa and Carlos' teen brother, Ricardo, jumped to their feet, yelling. Mama rose too, blowing him kisses. The Good News Club kids were nearly shrieking themselves hoarse. The applause hit Carlos like joy-filled thunder.

And after letting the din go on for awhile, Greg called for quiet again. "I've already cleared what I'm about to say with his parents, but he doesn't know yet."

A chuckle escaped the man. Carlos stared at the trainer. *I don't know what?*

Greg went on. "These two worked as hard as anybody I've ever seen," he said. "But it's more than that. He and Peppy just *gel,* you know? Now, Carlos has his heart set on entering Peppy in obedience trial competitions. But those things cost money that a kid his age doesn't have."

He placed his large hand on Carlos' right shoulder. *"So,* Carlos, how would you like to become my Saturday dog-training class assistant? I'll cover the cost of your competitions, as payment."

An expectant silence hung over the ball field. The boy was so stunned he couldn't respond right away. And then, all he could do was squeak, "For *real?"*

Everybody laughed.

"For real!"

"Yeah!" The boy felt like he was smiling all over. *Thank You, God,* he prayed. *Thank You, thank You!*

Greg dismissed everybody after one final applause. Carlos' classmates shook his hand and clapped his shoulders and patted Peppy. Becky gave him a hug. Carlos made sure he complimented the other owners, too. Then he hustled to help Greg pull out the ring stakes and wrap up the ribbon. "Roxy and I will pick you up next Saturday at nine o'clock," Greg told him as he climbed into his Chevy Suburban.

He kept the driver's-side door open and leaned out to give parting shots to both of them. First Peppy. "We're gonna get *you* to stop being so friendly to the figure eight assistants!" Then Carlos. "I saw you fidgeting with your left hand during the long down. You nearly gave him an extra hand signal, didn't you?"

Carlos' face flushed hot. "I—uh, yeah. But I *didn't.*"

"And it's a good thing because if you had, I would have docked you over half the points. You wouldn't have earned the qualifying score. Remember that when you're competing in a real obedience trial."

The boy's knees felt weak. *Guess Greg* was *watching!* He assured the man he'd never forget it.

Greg smiled. "I know you won't."

He turned his attention back to Peppy. "There's never been a perfect score given at any obedience trial I've ever attended. And I've been going to 'em for fifteen years. But *you,* my boy, may be the first!"

Peppy stepped in close and nosed Greg's hand. "Uh huh! Con artist!" he said, stroking the dog's ears. "Trying to soften up your coach so he'll go easier on you!"

He left laughing. Carlos was grinning too. He'd hardly stopped since graduation ended.

The three graduates hustled their dogs toward the parking lot so they could load them in Stan's truck for the trip home. "Stan!" shouted Ricardo as he jumped into the open back of the Hernandez pickup. It was already full of Good News Club kids. "How many points did Charlie get?"

Stan rolled his eyes and grinned. "Three! At least he didn't get zero!"

The kids cheered, including Carlos, but he couldn't keep himself from snickering, too. "Like *Kipsy*. I peeked at the score sheets!"

Becky gave him a disapproving glance, and he laughed harder. He suddenly broke into a run, and Peppy galloped alongside him. "We'll beat 'em to the truck, okay?"

They reached the royal-blue rig and stopped, panting. Carlos could hardly wait to go on with Peppy's training—to see him earn the titles of Companion Dog and Companion Dog Excellent. "And we don't gotta *wait,*" he told him. "In fact, we *can't.* We gotta be ready for the obedience trial coming up this spring!"

Peppy didn't seem worried. He leaped backwards, begging his young master to wrestle with him. Which he was only too happy to do. Mama leaned out the truck window and let the whole park know what *that dog* could do to Carlos' dress clothes.

And the boy loved every minute of it.

Get a Life!

This life is short, you know—and full of trouble. That's because *we all* have a problem called sin. We do bad things that break God's laws, like lying, cheating and having mean thoughts. And because God is holy—He never does wrong—sin keeps us away from Him. That's a bad situation because the punishment for sin is to be away from God *forever*.

But there's a good side. The Bible says, "God so loved the world that he gave his one and only Son, that whoever believes in him shall not perish but have eternal life" (John 3:16). God loves *you*. That's why Jesus Christ, God's Son, died on the cross to pay for *your* sins. Three days after they buried Him, He came back to life and today He's in Heaven. That's where He wants *you* to be someday. When you trust Him to save you from your sins, He does it. Would you like Jesus to forgive you right now? Go ahead and talk to Him. You can pray something like this:

Dear God, I believe You sent Jesus to die for me. I'm sorry for the wrong things I've done. Please take away my sin and help me live a new life. Thank You for being my absolutely best, Forever Friend. Amen.

If you just trusted Jesus to save you, you have a new life inside you. This would be a great time to join a Good News Club to learn more about your new life. Call 1-800-300-4033 to find out more.